CALIXTHE BEYALA was born in Cameroon, the sixth of a family of twelve children. She spent her childhood and adolescence in the shanty-town of New-Bell in Douala.

Now living in Paris, where she gained her degree, Beyala is a full-time writer and has enjoyed much success with her novels: *C'est le soleil qui m'a brûlée*, *Tu t'appelleras Tanga* and *Seul le diable savait* as well as *Le petit prince de Belleville*, here translated into English for the first time.

A firm supporter of women's liberation, Calixthe Beyala describes herself as having *'une passion: L'Afrique'*.

MARJOLIJN de JAGER has a PhD in Romance Languages and Literatures from the University of North Carolina – Chapel Hill. She presently lives in New York where she teaches French at the Beacon High School. Her translations from both the French and the Dutch are numerous and have won many plaudits. She gives her special interest as francophone African literature, particularly written by women.

I0743837

CALIXTHE BEYALA

LOUKOUM

The 'Little Prince' of Belleville

Translated from the French by
Marjolijn de Jager

Heinemann

Heinemann Educational Publishers
A Division of Heinemann Publishers (Oxford) Ltd
Halley Court, Jordan Hill, Oxford OX2 8EJ

Heinemann: A Division of Reed Publishing (USA) Inc.
361 Hanover Street, Portsmouth, NH 03801–3912, USA

Heinemann Educational Books (Nigeria) Ltd
PMB 5205, Ibadan

Heinemann Educational Boleswa
PO Box 10103, Village Post Office, Gaborone, Botswana

FLORENCE   PRAGUE   PARIS   MADRID
ATHENS   CHICAGO   MELBOURNE   JOHANNESBURG
AUCKLAND   SINGAPORE   TOKYO   SAO PAULO

First published in 1992 by Editions Albin Michel S.A. as *Le Petit Prince de Belleville*
First published by Heinemann Educational Publishers in 1995

British Library Cataloguing in Publication Data
A catalogue record for this book is available from the British Library.

ISBN 0435 909 681

Cover design by Touchpaper
Cover illustration by Jane Human
Author photograph by S. Haskell

Phototypeset by CentraCet Limited, Cambridge
Printed and bound in Great Britain
by Cox & Wyman Ltd, Reading, Berkshire

95 96 97 98 99 8 7 6 5 4 3 2 1

Culture is for everyone.

Whether they like it or not.

Education is OBLIGATORY.

And so it is that, little by little, others come to disturb us. To lend my son to authorities other than my own – to men and women whom I do not know but who are qualified to teach, so they tell me. And so the child breaks away from me. All I can do is to accept this, to sign report cards describing his weaknesses and his progress. It is a strange civilisation, one that judges a child according to criteria and grades by which his intelligence is coded.

The magic of contradictory reasoning escapes me.

I have given this business a great deal of thought.

I no longer recognise visible reflexions.

Each new day feeds my haggard eyes.

Other words take shape to oppose my own.

The jargon of generations of those people who control knowledge and science.

And what about my soul? Oh well, my soul clings to unattainable voyages.

In a bad way because of exile's poison.

I belong so very little to this world that I prefer to surrender.

(Abdou Traoré, Loukoum's revered father)

My name is Mamadou Traoré according to my birth certificate; in everyday use it is Loukoum. On official documents I am seven years old, but in Africa I would be ten seasons old. That was just so I wouldn't be put back in school. Besides, I am the tallest in my class, the strongest as well. Quite normal, since black people are stronger than anyone. That's the way it is. I live at 92, rue Jean-Pierre-Timbaud, up on the fifth floor, without a lift. There's a whole lot of us at home and if you know the area you'll also know that it's always full of African tribes living together in large groups without neglecting anyone. Solidarity is compelling.

I've always been a good boy. So give me an indication if you want to know what's happening with me. This autumn, after father left for work, I heard the mothers quarrelling.

The mothers? Right! I have two of them, and they are the cause of this whole row! Of course you know about it! It was in the newspapers. A nigger with two wives and a slew of kids just so he could receive family benefits for his dependants. It created a whole scene! I was worn out! But for God's sake! How was I supposed to know that everyone else only has one wife and that kids only have one mother? I thought, of course, that the children at school also had two of them but I never asked any questions since there wasn't any need to discuss it.

But I'd better begin at the beginning and tell you why the mothers were quarrelling. It was because I didn't know how to read and the teacher, Mademoiselle Garnier, had cornered me right away, as they always do.

They're funny these teachers, I don't know how it works but they're all the same. They always ask you the same questions and when you want to explain to them that we are taught the Koran, and that the Koran contains all there is to know on earth, and that father gets Allah's advice, and that I don't need to learn anything anyway because it's the women who'll be doing the work for me, they look at each other, shake their heads, and say:

'Oh! How awful. The poor kid!'

Still, Mademoiselle Garnier asked me where I lived exactly, what my father and my mother did, if I knew how to read and write and all that stuff and when I answered: 'Of course I know how to read,' she brought me the book in question, just to check me out. An amazing book it was, by the way, at least from what I was able to grasp. It talked about a kid, a little prince, who sees a hat that becomes a snake and that was cool. What I wouldn't give to get my hands on that book

2

again to find out how it ends . . . If you know anything about it, write to me at the above address.

To get back to Mademoiselle Garnier, when she saw how much trouble I was having with the book, she adjusted her glasses, looked at me, and said:

'Hm . . . hm . . . I thought so!'

True, it didn't go like clockwork. It wasn't so much that the words were difficult, but the guy who wrote it had words a mile long, words that went on and on and on.

'Mamadou, you should have told me you didn't know how to read. Didn't your parents ever tell you that a little boy shouldn't tell lies?'

'First of all, I'm not a little boy. And then, I do know how to read, Mademoiselle. Only this thing has weird writing!'

'You dare to insinuate that Saint-Exupéry hadn't mastered the basic rules of French grammar?'

'I don't know the guy. But I know one thing, his stuff is put together in a strange way and nobody can make any sense of it. Look, I'll make you see.'

I had chewing gum in my mouth. I stuck it out on the tip of my tongue and blew a bubble. It snapped *pop!* and then I went to the blackboard and wrote.

'Look,' I said to her, pointing to what I had written, 'look at that: *Wa ilâhoun Wâhid, lâ ilâha illâ houwa rahmânou-rahim.*'

She stopped me there and did she let me have it! She wouldn't believe I was actually reading. Yet I told her that it was written there, right under her nose, that 'Your God is the only God, there is no other God than he, generous and merciful.'

'You see,' I told her, 'it's you who doesn't understand anything.'

Then she went: 'Well, that's the limit!'

She'd had enough. She said it was shameful for a boy not to be able to read anything but the Koran, that it was contrary to the French lifestyle, and that she was going to alert the school inspector and have me put in a special school. Of course, that didn't appeal to me but there was nothing I could do and I had to wait till my dad was done with his rubbish collecting.

The fact remains that schoolkids are nasty and they began to get rowdy and yell: 'He doesn't know how to read! ha! ha!' And it made me sick to hear all those kids carry on. If that isn't sad, to be so intolerant. After school, M'am came to pick me up. Then we had what you might call a conference with the teacher, then with the Principal, and it was getting M'am all hot and bothered, so she told them she was doing everything she could and wouldn't leave my side until I knew French perfectly.

Me, in my corner, I was trying to catch a few more lines of the book before they could take it away from me, and I asked M'am:

'Have you ever heard of Saint-Exupéry?'

'Yeah,' she answered. 'He's in the Koran, verse 18.'

When they heard that, they were all over her and that's when she remembered her stomach. She is a refined person, distinguished and all that. Only her stomach makes certain *gloo-gloc* sounds and every time that happens to her she puts her hand over her mouth and says: 'Excuse me.' It's no fun having to put up with something like that all day long. No fun at all. On top of that, she has a lump. About seven or eight years ago she had it taken out, together with some other things, and that idiot of a doctor could find nothing better to say than that it was the biggest and most beautiful tumour he had ever seen, besides the one that some other person, I don't remember who, had taken out of an elephant's womb. The fact is that M'am is so proud of this business that she brought the lump home, and put it in a large jar to show it to everyone. Once she opened the door (by mistake, of course) to a welfare worker and there was M'am, talking to her about her tumour for six hours straight without taking a breath. Finally, the young caseworker gave her some papers to fill out, saying she'd come to collect them after her holiday. Gradually, rather than spending their time avoiding M'am and instead of asking her: 'How are you feeling, Madame Abdou?', they ask: 'How is your tumour?' At which point M'am smiles broadly and says: 'Very well, thank you.' Then she slyly goes on to other things.

'Think about it,' she says to them, 'a tumour of seven kilos. Even our great men didn't weigh that much at birth. At the most they were three kilos. De Gaulle, Mitterrand, Alain Delon, Johnny Halliday, Mireille Mathieu, Dalida.'

At that point the Principal chokes a bit and says:

4

'I'm so sorry, Madame, but let's get back to your son.'

'My son? Ah, Monsieur, that boy, you have no idea. Always with his nose buried in books! All day long, Monsieur! At this rate he will soon know a whole lot more than a welfare worker.'

'Madame, let's be serious. If you want your son to be integrated into his class, it is time to take some action . . .'

'Don't say that, Monsieur. Do not say that, my good sir . . . That is racism! Pure and simple! Racism!'

'Madame . . .'

'Don't say anything more! Ah, who would have expected that!'

'Madame, every child here . . .'

'Not every child, Monsieur. Not every child . . . My little Loukoum is so sweet! Give him a chance and you won't regret it. Oh no!'

And M'am had tears in her eyes just because she was telling them how sweet I was.

All of which meant that they continued their discussion a while longer and finally they came to an agreement with M'am and allowed me to stay in Mademoiselle Garnier's class. But they warned her that if I didn't know how to read and write by the end of the term, they would send me to a special school in the district of Antony, and for good. In Antony, I thought . . . That seemed strange to me, seeing as we'd never set foot in that area, but I said nothing.

◆

We left the school. Outside the sky was overcast, all streaky, that is. It was going to rain. I saw the cloud coming. It was black and long and writhing so much that I couldn't tell where it was heading. We ran, but the storm caught us. So we took refuge in Monsieur Guillaume's café.

Monsieur Guillaume has small black eyes, with a hooked nose, and a salt and pepper beard that grows all over his face. His belly is as big as that of a pregnant woman and his bushy hair is beginning to turn grey. As soon as he sees us, his eyes become two minuscule slits of happiness as M'am asks:

'How's business, my dear, dear Guillaume?'

'Bad! Ever since the crisis began in this country it's not been going well at all. My business is down by half. The blacks don't go out any more, so . . .'

'That's bad luck,' M'am goes.

Monsieur Guillaume shakes his head like someone who doesn't understand anything and says:

'To top it all, the cops are everywhere which doesn't help matters. Providing they don't chase that one away from me, too,' he adds as he rolls his eyes to the left.

In the time it took us to look, the person Monsieur Guillaume was pointing out to us had got up. It was Monsieur Kaba.

Monsieur Kaba comes to us from Guinea. He is the best dressed gentleman you can imagine in Paris. He has pink shirts and fancy, expensive ties. He is the biggest pimp amongst the blacks in Belleville. He is accompanied by his bodyguard, Monsieur Richard Makossa, and by two girls. I know one of them very well. Her name is Tatiana. Of course she's not really a girl, considering she has falsies and she can't have kids. I don't know the other one. She has dyed red hair. She's wearing a kind of very short vest, with a belt and boots. She's terribly pretty. You can tell that Monsieur Guillaume finds her very cute.

Monsieur Kaba approaches us, both hands outstretched, his cigar in his mouth, and says:

'Look who's paying us a visit? Madame Abdou herself!'

He kisses M'am on both cheeks and asks:

'What beautiful things have you got to tell me about, my dear?'

'Nothing in particular, my friend . . . And how about you? Everything OK?'

'Yeah . . . except for the fascists who're a pain in the neck. They want to get us out of here . . .'

'They won't succeed,' M'am goes. 'We're at home here. My husband is a veteran.'

'May God hear you, my darling . . . But let's talk about nicer things . . .'

He draws on his fat cigar before he carries on:

'I was thinking of visiting you one of these days . . . It's been a long time since I've eaten a good rice and fish dinner.'

'Whenever you want, my dear. You're always welcome. M'am is always there.'

'I know, I know,' he says. 'But how is good old Abdou? First of all, where is he?'

'At work.'

'Ah! If I had a wife like you, I wouldn't let her out of my sight for a minute! Not one minute!'

'Uncle, where is your wife?' I ask.

'In Africa.'

'And why aren't you with her? And where are your children? And why don't they live in France?'

He doesn't answer me. He lets his cigar droop out of his kisser and lets the ash drop all over the floor without thinking of the expense. Then he turns to M'am and says to her:

'Bright, that boy of yours.'

'Yeah.'

Monsieur Kaba shakes his head knowingly.

'He'll make something of himself later on. Some of the questions he asks! If he ever finds someone to answer him, he'll end up knowing more than any police inspector.'

◆

Monsieur Kaba goes back and sits down again. And he says to us:

'Come and join us for a bit.'

'Oh, no, no! This is no place for a w . . . I mean for . . .'

'Ah, my friend. What did I tell you?' (He turns to Makossa.) 'I told you! Take most of those godforsaken pink arses who spend their time getting fat at our expense; they sit around and don't lift a finger to earn their keep. But with these chicks, our own women, it's different. They wear themselves out for their poor guys, always busy fretting over what they'll feed them! It makes your heart proud to know they're always on the go.'

The two girls who were sitting at his table looked at each other, couldn't have looked more serious, but you can tell they're having the hardest time in the world not to snigger. Then all of a sudden Tatiana begins to chuckle, the girl with the red hair does too. Then, of course, they both burst out laughing. Like hyenas, they're laughing so hard they have to hold on to each other.

Tatiana wipes her eyes.

'That's the end!' Tatiana goes.

At that point she doubles up and starts laughing all over again. They're leaning up against the wall and are having a ball. People must hear them a mile away.

'You see that!' says Monsieur Kaba. 'Sin and corruption are tearing the earth apart!'

He falls silent, frowns, raises one finger and continues:

'The hour will come, I warn you! Armageddon isn't far off! It will crush all of you!'

'Who's that, Armageddon?' I ask M'am.

'I haven't the slightest. But what's sure is that he will pass him by.'

Just then the redhead gets up.

'Where are you off to?' asks Monsieur Kaba.

She doesn't answer, looks as if she doesn't give a royal fuck. She pulls out a stool and sits down at the bar.

'Hey you . . .' goes Monsieur Kaba. 'It's time for work, you aren't forgetting that, I hope?'

She looks around, then answers:

'Besides these bipeds here, I don't see a soul. If someone who is somebody should show up, let me know.'

'I was just listening to the radio,' Monsieur Guillaume says. 'It seems they've never seen anything like it since the exodus of the Kurds.'

'Shit! Shit!' Monsieur Kaba cries out. 'I did what I had to do as soon as I knew. You can really feel the Arab competition. So now if the Rumanians are also getting into it, we've had it.'

'You don't have to carry on like that,' says Monsieur Guillaume. 'With the chick you just dug up, you should be able to have a fine old time. Ha! Ha! You can boast about your vices.'

'Oh, shut up!' goes the redhead.

Monsieur Guillaume's eyes open as wide as two saucers. He opens his mouth and nothing comes out but *ffft . . . tsss . . .* I have the impression he's either laughing or choking, which it is remains to be seen.

'Hey, old man,' she starts again. 'Put your tongue back in or you're going to wet the front of your shirt.'

Monsieur Kaba looks at her.

8

'Esther, I think I've told you before not to talk that way to guys.'

'All right, all right,' she answers. 'I'm bored to death in here.'

Then she lights a cigarette, takes a drag, looks at her legs and raises her eyes to Monsieur Guillaume.

'So, what's the problem, grandpa? Do I have pimples somewhere?'

'Eh? Eh . . . No. For a minute I thought we'd met before.'

'That would surprise me!'

'Cool it,' Monsieur Kaba says looking at Monsieur Guillaume. 'Esther belongs to one of the oldest aristocratic families in France. She's a sensitive young girl whose fiancé was killed in a car accident. You must understand she's a little touchy.'

'Poor little thing,' says Monsieur Guillaume. 'I'm really sorry about your fiancé. Here you're amongst family and you can count on any one of us, isn't that so, guys?'

'Yeah!' the others respond.

Mademoiselle Esther yawns and says:

'Just what I need.'

At that point, M'am takes me by the arm, raises her hand, and says:

'See you later everybody!'

'Stay a little while,' says Monsieur Kaba.

'Have a drink,' Monsieur Guillaume suggests.

'Got to go, have to get dinner ready and a lot else to do besides. But why don't you come by one of these days and I'll make you a nice rice and fish dinner?'

'Love to, Madame Abdou,' goes Monsieur Kaba.

We left.

Outside the storm was waiting for us. The rain was falling on the cars like little electric rays and making a lot of noise. We were about five hundred yards from home. We turned a corner and ended up on rue Jean-Pierre-Timbaud. M'am was walking ahead without a word.

'She's beautiful, Mademoiselle Esther,' I told her. 'Do you believe she's an aristocrat?'

'That would amaze me.'

'Me too. But she does have the manners of a classy girl.'

You would have thought M'am didn't hear me. She suddenly stops in front of the door to our building and says as if to herself:

'Whore!'

9

Look out for yourself! Look out for yourself! Steal! Pillage! The main point? Don't get caught.

I know these words. They keep me company and keep the abyss at a safe distance from me. They unleash my weariness and fill me with dreams. They come and go inside my head like a ball between my hands. They use me up, exhaust me, but I cling to them as if to a bit of earth, a bush.

I can tell you everything. I've met so many men and women who came in droves to cling on to the city. Paris. An image, a perfume, a sunless mirage, without trees.

In my sleepless hours, I roam the streets, the alleyways. The night girds my loins with solitude and undresses my memory. In it, I hear the noises of a forgotten city melting away, a faraway rumble, a breath that falls silent, and the silence of chasms settling in. Nothing here, nobody here, everything is absent in the interior night where the friend is resting and who, then, would keep watch? Me. My ghosts. My land.

And what if it were an honour to be waiting in the night, toppled down by time, and what if the dark night heralded radiant gardens? What if the shadow, suddenly criss-crossed by lightning, were to be torn open to reveal the promised day?

I am still waiting. Twenty years. Twenty years as long as sadness itself.

And yet, down there on that land that no longer belongs to us, the drums used to murmur. Mouths would whisper hope: Money, money! It is there, in that transparent country across the seas, amidst the cars, the candelabras, and the cracked walls . . . Mouths would say: There's money, millions to be gathered, everywhere, with your hands, with your head, with your heart, with your behind . . . You'd have to look out for yourself. Look out for yourself!

10

Fortune has opened its wings, exile has begun.

I came to this country in the grip of material gain, expelled from my own land by need. I came, we came to this country to save our skin, to buy our children a future. I arrived, we arrived in bundles with a hope as enormous as memory itself, hidden deep in our hearts.

(*Abdou Traoré*)

When we came home, my dad was sitting in front of the television. He looked at us, then changed the channel. I sat down next to him.

'Is it true that the fascists want us out of here?' I asked him.

'Be quiet!'

Then he focused on what was happening on the screen. I don't like the news. But the broadcast wouldn't stop. I put my hands over my eyes so I wouldn't see. First, people are climbing on a roadblock in an area from which they're going to chase away the Indians who've been living there forever. Then they're going to make a film about the guy who murdered a lot of old ladies. And the same actor is playing the judge and the murderer. And do you know what they're going to do to the delegate who stole all that money? Absolutely nothing!

The best part is waiting for Inspector Malcom who comes on after the news. He's so smart that he always wins in the end.

When it's over, there he goes, my dad, turning off the television. Even though I didn't get to see Inspector Malcom. Then he rolled a colanut between his hands. He peeled off the skin. He bit into it. He chewed it, then said:

'Some nerve he's got, that Le Pen, wanting to make us believe that if things are a mess in France it's because of us. As if to say we're not shrewd enough to get by. That we came here to have a picnic off their plates. That guy really is depraved, a blunderer, and he's not even lucky. Let me tell you: me, I'm a veteran. This Le Pen hadn't even been born when I was defending France. In the trenches of Algeria I was. Hell on wheels, my boy! You can, oh no, you can't imagine what it was like! The heat, the mosquitoes, the sickness, and the bullets flying. And what if I'd died, eh? Who for, eh, tell me that?'

I didn't answer. My dad went *pfff . . . pfff . . .* Then, with pursed

11

lips he spat out the colanut juice like an arrow which just cleared the windowsill and landed in the courtyard with a plop!

'For France! Long live France! Long live the French!'

'Is he really awful, Dad, Le Pen?'

'Yeah! With Nazis you can expect just about anything! Heh, heh!'

'What's that, a Nazi?'

'A dangerous man. A raging madman.'

'But Dad, there's the police. They're stronger than anyone. They'll put him in jail.'

'Don't count on it, son! The cops work for those who pay them. We bust a gut trying to find some way to pay our taxes so that these fat slobs can lounge around at City Hall. Not even one single straight cop! At that rate, they're pushing us miserable wretches into doing desperate things and running for elections.'

I mull this over and say:

'There's Mitterrand, Daddy, he's your friend.'

He doesn't answer. So I insist:

'He even gave you your residence papers.'

'Yeah,' he goes.

'So?'

He frowns and looks at me. I stay quiet, then I say:

'You could write to him. He's more powerful than anyone. So then nobody will kick us out.'

In my head the letter is already written, but I can't compose it in French for reasons you already know. It could go like this:

Mr President,

First, I offer my condolences for the unfair competition that has come knocking at your door.

Allow me to tell you that you have my full support and that, at the first sign from you, I shall throw myself heart and soul into an assault on the enemy, striking him when he's right in the middle of his meeting. Mankind surely is most ungrateful to his Lord. You are an eyewitness to this. He is also most attached to the material goods of this world. Does he really not know that when the graves are turned over and when the balance sheet of what is inside men's hearts is drawn up, on that day the Lord will be completely informed about them?

Monsieur Le Pen, our mortal enemy, claims he will run all of us out of here. But I know that you, who know all that is invisible as well as what is visible, you alone deserving of the finest tributes, you won't let him make his vile plan a reality.

My father, whom you undoubtedly know since you gave him his papers in the year 1981 as you became the supreme magistrate, is a veteran infantryman of France. But in case you don't remember this, please know that he is a tall chap with grey hair, insofar as he still has any. He is skinnier than anyone else and when he looks in the mirror, he opens his eyes as if he doesn't see himself. On Saturdays and Sundays he is dressed to kill. He puts on a suit with all his war medals and spends his time on the boulevard Ménilmontant. When he's not on duty collecting rubbish, he does floor exercises to gain weight, but he doesn't gain any because of his daily worries. All this is just to tell you that he bothers no one and eats almost nothing. As for the Jews and the Arabs, I can't speak for them. As for the Negroes, I can assure you they are in no way, absolutely no way at all, exactly like my dad. It's not Monsieur Le Pen's fault if he suffers from misinformation, for social separation makes all people stay in their own district without intending any harm. So I'm suggesting to you that you organise a committee whose goal it would be to do a census on Negroes in distress, especially those stuck in maids' rooms without an elevator, who aren't able to give any sign of their presence except by having wild parties. There are so many of them who are illegal residents and unemployed, that it would nail the mouth of the President of the National Front shut.

In the hope that you will respond favourably to my request, I am

very truly yours,
devotedly, Loukoum

As you already know, I can't write it all by myself since French has the annoying habit of having endlessly long words. So I looked my dad straight in the eye and said:

'So?'

'What, Loukoum?'

'You'll write to him, uh, say you will, dad?'

He looks at me, bites into a piece of colanut, and turns towards the kitchen.

'Are we going to be allowed to eat in this house today?'

◆

The next morning is when they made the scene. M'am asks me what I want for breakfast.

'Well, first of all, what is there?'

'Bread, cereal, jam, butter, tea, milk, coffee.'

'That's all? No porridge, bean fritters, or corn?'

I begin to laugh. Her stomach goes *gloo-gloc* and she says: 'Excuse me.'

And I laugh again.

'No,' I say. 'I don't want all that junk. Just give me a bowl of milk, please.'

She doesn't argue. She's wearing her white nightgown, since she was on matrimonial duty last night. I think it looks pretty, her skinny black hand coming out of the sleeve. But at the same time M'am frightens me with her veins, some so thin and others so swollen. Something is pushing me towards her. Just for a moment, I'd gladly take that hand to warm my icy fingers, but I don't do it because I'm a man.

'May I sit next to you to drink my tea?' she asks me.

I say of course, showing it doesn't bother me. She opens a magazine. There are plenty of white women in it. Some are laughing and making their coats swirl. Others are singing on the bonnet of a car. Some are riding bicycles and waving goodbye. M'am is turning the pages. But she looks unhappy, like a kid who didn't get its toy. So she closes the magazine and throws it across the room.

She drinks her tea and attacks a slice of plantain cake she baked herself. When she makes it, you can smell it for miles around. This one perfumed the house in no time at all. She spreads jam on a slice of bread. She bites into it, gives me a sly look and says:

'Don't you want a bit of it, son?'

14

I hesitate a moment, then I say no. But you can see that I'm dying to have some. She shrugs her shoulders and drinks a big gulp of her tea.

Someone is calling her.

We look up at the same time. It's Soumana. She has a toothpick that never leaves her. She pushes it to her other cheek and asks:

'Can I talk to you?'

'Right now?'

'It can't wait.'

'All right.'

M'am gets up, puts her chair back in place, and follows her to the kitchen.

So I throw myself on the cake and eat a small bit, just enough for it not to be noticeable. You could say a mouse had stopped by. I was calmly drinking my bowl of milk when I heard screaming!

'It's your fault! And now we have to pay for private lessons for Loukoum . . . Oh no! I've sacrificed enough like this . . . And it's all your doing! Too much, it's just too much. I can't take this. Anyway, where will you find the money?'

'My fault? My fault was to have welcomed you into my house. After all Abdou didn't force you to sleep with him!'

'Oh yes, it is your fault!'

'Sure . . . The children weren't born yet. All you had to do was leave right away . . .'

I put everything down and run to see what's going on. I hide right behind the curtain. I know that if they find me there, I'm sure to get a thrashing for having spied. I'm curious to know what's making them scream at each other like this. Soumana turns her back to me.

'I couldn't,' she said. 'I couldn't go away. Leave! Like a rag that's good for nothing any more! My mother entrusted me to you! You didn't do anything to protect me. Nothing! It suited you fine that I stepped into your place because at the time you weren't interested in it. You didn't even do anything when I cried out for help, I was in pain. And when I was pregnant the first time, you didn't say anything either. You closed your eyes with my second pregnancy. The third time you yelled at me all the time. And you haven't stopped hurling abuse at me. Time to set the table, and the food was cold. Time to get breakfast ready and it was already time for lunch. You never had

15

anything else to say. Never. Today you have nothing to say to me either. Nothing at all. Nothing.'

M'am shrugs her shoulders and drops them. She sighs. She looks tired and sad. She says:

'It's never too late, I'm not throwing you out. But if you really want to leave . . . Nobody will know a thing. The children don't understand yet. It's up to you.'

'No, m'lady, never!' screams Soumana, looking mean. 'You hate my children . . . I've seen how you eye them when you think nobody's looking . . . And now you have to pay for classes for Loukoum . . . With what money, at whose expense, may I ask? That of my own children.'

'Loukoum is your son, too.'

'He's nobody's son here, except his father's. Nobody here suffered belly-aches for him. He came out of nobody's slit . . . You know that as well as I do.'

'That doesn't matter to me,' says M'am. 'I got him when he was very little, when he was still sucking his thumb. It was the gift heaven sent me since I've never been pregnant beyond the first few months even once.'

'Pull the wool over your own eyes if you want. The truth is you're just like Abdou, the only thing you're interested in is the child benefit. I don't buy that story!'

It was then that it dawned on me. I hadn't known that M'am wasn't my mum. I felt as if an iron was twisting my entrails and I clutched on to the curtain, closed my eyes, and breathed hard, very hard. I felt such pain . . .

'Loukoum!' I hear someone cry.

'Loukoum!'

'It's your fault!'

'No, it's yours!'

'They're MY children. And if it turns sour, I'll take them with me.'

Then there was a long silence. M'am looks at Soumana as if she hasn't understood what she has just said. Then she says in a very calm voice:

'You seem to be forgetting one thing, which is that officially I am the mother of these children . . . We are in France here.'

'In that case I'm going to tell all.'

'Yeah, that's it . . . Go ahead . . . Go snitch wherever you want, Judas . . . But I'll tell you one thing, you can't get out of it that way . . . My word! Allah isn't blind. The air itself can testify to how I've lived with you.'

I don't know what to do, I feel like crying, but tears are traitors, they're never there when you need them. So I go to the window, I lean my head out and look down the street. It's sunny. There's no school. I'm thinking that it's a good day to go to the park to toboggan. But I don't feel like it, I feel like nothing at all, I'm at my very lowest.

'Loukoum,' goes M'am, trying to take me into her arms.

I recoiled, I felt like killing someone, which is not like me, I felt like doing something that wasn't right.

'Loukoum, you are my son, it doesn't make any difference.'

'No!'

I pushed her aside, ran off, opened the door, and flew downstairs.

◆

Despite the sun, it was cold outside. I continued to run and it took me a while to realise that it was cold and that I wasn't wearing a lot of clothes. And I found myself in Monsieur Guillaume's café again.

Monsieur Laforêt is there. Monsieur Laforêt is French and comes from the sixteenth *arrondissement*. He used to be a managing director somewhere, but after his dismissal he came to Belleville. His eyes look kindly upon the world around him and have seen everything. So I sat down across from him and looked at his face . . . He looks sad and tired. I notice his chin goes right in. He hardly has one. I have more of a chin than he does. His clothes are very dirty. When he leans forward you can smell him. He smiles and I ask:

'Monsieur Laforêt, how come you're still smiling?'

'It's a habit, Loukoum.'

He is silent and then says:

'Before, when I was a young director, I had plenty of friends. In the evening after work, we'd go out for dinner, we'd go to a nightclub, we used to have a fine time. When I lost my job my wife left me, my children left, my friends disappeared. I have nobody any more. Nobody stuck up for me . . .'

17

He looks at the wall and I notice his eyes are a little wet.

Monsieur Guillaume comes over to us. He's wearing overalls over a shirt. His little black eyes seem to shine as he looks at us, a bit like a seal.

'You all right, Loukoum?' asks Monsieur Guillaume.

'Yeah.'

'No school today?'

'It's Wednesday . . .'

'Of course, of course! I'm getting old. Heh, heh! In my time we had Thursday off. It was my favourite day when I was young. I never did understand a thing of what she talked about, Madame Goodman. She said the earth was round but I think it's as flat as a pancake.'

He laughs a bit, then pulls a yellow handkerchief from his overalls. A kind of black powder falls out of it. He looks at it, stunned.

'Honestly,' he says as if to himself, 'how did that pepper get in there? Oh yeah, I remember now, I spilled some at breakfast. Atchoo!'

I get it full in the face and sneeze. Then it's Monsieur Laforêt's turn. But only he has tears in his eyes.

Monsieur Guillaume sneezes some more and says:

'Bloody pepper, really!'

He looks at Monsieur Laforêt, then asks:

'How about a drink?'

He goes to the bar, returns with a glass of wine and puts it in front of Monsieur Laforêt. He pulls up a chair, sits down, and stretches his legs.

'You never know,' he says, 'this could be a great remedy. Even if it doesn't much help you get a job, it sure will stop you thinking about it.'

Slowly Monsieur Laforêt turns his head and says in a sad voice:

'You don't understand. I love Caroline. I've always loved her and I will always love her. I can't forget her just like that.'

'Well now,' says Monsieur Guillaume, 'and screw up your whole life just like that!' (Here Monsieur Laforêt groans.) 'She didn't hesitate for a second to drop you at the first sign of hardship.'

'That makes no difference to me . . .'

'And what about that young lover she has now?' (He shakes his

18

head as if he were thinking of something very serious.) 'It remains to be seen if those three kids are really yours, pal.'

'I'll tell you one thing for sure and that's that all Caroline's children are mine. That I can swear to!'

Monsieur Guillaume clears his throat.

'Listen to me carefully, if you've decided to be a bum and a drunk because a woman has left you in the lurch, that's up to you!'

'It's not Caroline who left me, it's society.'

'Listen, old man, I really feel for you. There aren't many men who'd continue to love their wife under these circumstances. But here you are, it can't be helped, all you have to do now is snap out of it.'

Monsieur Guillaume got up, our eyes met. He coughed and said to me:

'Just go upstairs, your friend Alex is up there. He's with a new buddy. Hurry up and join him. This is no place for a kid.'

I didn't hesitate for a second. I had my own share of problems and was quite upset enough. I wasn't going to explain to them all of a sudden that I'd immigrated just for family welfare payments. So, I went around the bar and climbed up the stairs four at a time to join my friend Alex.

No, friend, stop firing words at me that hurt, stop weighing me in your hand like three kilos of lost sunlight. Listen and try to understand. Bearing a beautiful first name gives one self-confidence in life – Bearing the same family name as those who have been dead for ages helps to give a direction to our lives – Giving your last name to your descendants is the best way of defying your own death. I've been defeated. Would you like to see me fall even lower, without the air bearing witness to what has been?

At the border patrol you registered my body and wrapped it in contempt, in hatred. In your wide-open eyes I was already suspected of rape or of murder. Obsessed with sex. A pile of mud charged with obstructing memories and propagating AIDS.

We're living in a double world; I know it, you know it, as one would speak of a double meaning or a double life. We're walking parallel lines, acrobats on the tightrope that separates us, between two chasms of opposite realities. Day overshadows night. And the nights awaken the silences of the day. In the end, however, day should win out and we should create light.

Woman, you know, is an ambiguous creature. Her magnificent vagina opens up at our song and her lips of sun cause the promises of morning to rise straight up to the horizon. She is there, present and precise in the mist, delineating rays, indicating the trees on the plain. Then, at the first moments of sunlight, she becomes ebony pink and more blurred. A cloth of dreams that comes unwound in our bedrooms and wraps us up in the rough fabric of lies.

(Abdou Traoré)

20

I've known Alex since I was born. We're both in Mademoiselle Garnier's class. Alex is the youngest kid ever expelled from school. He used to beat other children up so badly that when he was four years old the teacher threw him out of school with the order not to return again. Monsieur Guillaume ought to have paid her off, and I really mean that too, but he would smile at her in ways he didn't want to have to smile, just so she would take back her command, like the cops when they're writing you a ticket and you know them. But despite all of this we are brothers. Not real brothers, of course, but foster brothers as they say down there in Africa, which I don't know if I've pointed out. When we were little kids and bawling, M'am could find no better solution than to give us her breasts, dried up though they might be. All we had to do was close our mouths.

To tell you the truth, nobody knows who Alex's parents are. He's a little coloured boy from Social Services being brought up as if he's white. Monsieur Guillaume adopted him and raised him without any problems until his wife, a big black woman, died of something. They couldn't have any kids. Monsieur Guillaume is raising him without asking himself too many questions. He doesn't even know whether Alex is Malian, Cameroonian or Senegalese. But it means a lot to him that Alex spends time with black people so he won't lose the habit. Usually on Friday evenings after school, Alex comes home with me and everybody is pleased to see a little white boy who is really black. A kind of zebra really! Looking at him, my dad always says that he'd swear he's the child of a white man and a goddamn negress. My dad gives him his religion so that he won't let go of the Koran, for even if he were to stay in France until his dying day, he should remember that he has a country somewhere; he shouldn't break with Allah, even if it doesn't count for much here. Monsieur Guillaume doesn't let things alone. He says that for him the colour of someone's skin doesn't count. He says that all people are equal, except for the arseholes, and that if blacks beat each other up it's because they think they're different. All this is just to explain to you that Monsieur Guillaume respects other people's beliefs. Sometimes Monsieur Guillaume pays a visit to Monsieur Ousmane, the marabout of the rue Bisson, to solve his problems. When he comes back, his eyes are all shiny. Eyes are the windows of the soul, my dad says. When you're sad, it's in your eyes. M'am adds

21

that eyes are sad 'cause they're looking for mistakes. But I can swear to you that I don't understand a thing, not anything at all. I'm so sad that I'd like to die, because my mothers aren't my mums. Yet I have my two eyes, I see as clearly as you do. I keep looking for my mistake but it's no use, I don't see it. So if you can explain this to me, I'm at your disposal.

Alex is much more gifted than me. Sometimes he explains things to me, but I have a hard time understanding what he's explaining. It just won't stay put inside my skull because I have too many memories, and it's overflowing inside up there. It's like a cupboard really! He says things like it's the clouds that bring the rain or that there are planets much larger than the earth, that the earth is round, all of that, or that the stars are bigger than the moon. I just say: 'Oh, really.' Personally, I find stars to be as minuscule as two tears.

I went upstairs to find out what you're supposed to do when you discover your mothers aren't your mothers.

Alex is wearing blue striped pyjamas. He opens the door and mutters something since he's happy to see me. There's a kid crying somewhere, but I don't know where it's coming from.

Alex looks at me and says: 'Come, so I can introduce someone to you.'

I follow him. While we're walking, he tells me:

'He'll be your neighbour soon because his mother works for Monsieur Kaba and can't take care of him. So, it's your neighbour, Madame Zola, who'll be taking him in as a lodger.'

Finally we get to his bedroom and he opens the door. There's a kid in there with a very runny nose, crouched on the floor. But he's wearing his Sunday clothes, with a tie and a white shirt.

'I have the honour of introducing the Pink Panther of Belleville to you. Careful, he scratches.'

Me, I'm just watching, I don't dare move.

'Come closer,' he says. 'He won't eat you. He scratches, that's all.'

He goes out and leaves me alone with the Pink Panther of Belleville and his scratching. For the moment, he is quiet, the snot in his nose running into his mouth, which he swallows as if it were cream. But my heart is beating, beating a mile a minute. Then, suddenly, he shows his claws, he jumps up, he shrieks, then stops and looks at me in a funny

22

way. I'm all shaken up so I smile faintly, not showing my hand. Then he goes to the cupboard that stands crammed in right behind the door. He takes out some clothes and throws them on the floor. He looks around. His eyes are rolling in their sockets. Then he starts to tear up the clothes.

'That's not allowed,' I say to him, 'you shouldn't ruin clothes.'

He says nothing in return.

'You shouldn't dirty your clothes and you shouldn't destroy them,' I repeat. 'If you don't stop doing that, Monsieur Guillaume will really take a swipe at you. And besides, it's not good to eat your snot,' I add.

He doesn't answer.

Somebody is trying to open the door. Gently at first. Then with such force that it shoves Timothée, who is stuck behind it, backwards. I no longer see him at all. Monsieur Guillaume comes in:

'Can't you play without making noise?' he asks.

I open my mouth. Then remain shut up like a clam. He sees the clothes on the floor. His face turns as red as a beetroot.

'What's this bloody mess?'

He comes closer. He grabs my ears. He pulls hard to make me feel it and asks:

'Did you do this?' And then adds: 'Really, you can't trust a nigger.'

Suddenly he sees Timothée. He lets go of me. He grabs him by the hand. He tries to get him to come out of there. Then Timothée jumps up and scratches his chest. 'You dirty little bastard!' Monsieur Guillaume yells. He thumps him and leaves the room, grumbling to himself.

Timothée is calm, quieter than the rain. He gives me a funny look.

'You shouldn't scratch,' I tell him.

'Mummy, mummy,' he replies.

'That'll get you nowhere, calling for your mum like that,' I tell him. 'And anyway, you ought not to sit on the floor in your Sunday clothes.'

He looks at me without saying a word. His eyes are brown with flashes of grey in them, like a white person who's partly coloured has.

'Is your mum coming on Sunday?' I ask him.

He still doesn't answer. I can see in his eyes that he is in distress.

Monsieur Guillaume and Madame Zola arrived. Only Timothée isn't acting up any more. I simply told them:

'Leave him alone!'

They acted as if I hadn't spoken, as adults always do when they don't want to respond to something.

Madame Zola crouches down in front of Timothée and says:

'Be a good boy, Ti, today is Sunday and if you're not good, your mummy won't come to take you out for a walk.'

'It isn't Sunday,' I say. 'Today is Wednesday, Madame Zola.'

She turns round, looks at me. Only she doesn't look me in the eye. And then I add:

'It's not nice to lie to children.'

◆

Alex joined me again. He asked if I wanted anything to drink. I said no.

'Don't you want any gum?' he asked again.

'No,' I said.

'Something bugging you?'

So then I told him everything.

'That's really tough,' he said as he pulled a chair over.

Then he ran his hands through his frizzy hair, picked his nose and wiped it off on his pyjamas.

'How long have you known?'

'I just found out.'

'That's really something. What are you going to do?'

'Dunno. Sometimes I wonder why life is so complicated.'

"Cause it's life, of course,' he answered. 'Some people make it complicated just for fun.'

'No other reasons?'

'Well, sometimes people are just bored.'

'I didn't ask to be born.'

'Nobody does.'

'So?'

He had to think that over for a while and frowned.

'All I can tell you is that Africa's full of women who have kids without being married. So, they don't know what else to do except abandon them.'

24

'Maybe you're right. So you think she'll come looking for me?'

'Maybe yes, maybe no.'

He's quiet for a while, then says:

'Anyway, what the hell do you care if they're not your mothers, uh?'

'It's important, very important.'

'That's just snobbism, all that. They love you.'

'I'm not so sure.'

'You only have to look at how they are with you. Then decide. But if ever . . . I've got lots of addresses, just in case.'

◆

When I came back downstairs, the café was crowded. Some have very fine clothes. And others are not so wonderful. Then I see Esther. She's dressed the same as yesterday, only now it's a pair of little red shorts with boots to match. I say hello. She's very nice.

'It's the little guy from last night!' she goes, surprised. 'How are you?'

'Fine, m'am.'

She bends over towards me. She strokes my hair and says:

'You're so cute! I'd really love to have a little kid like you.'

'Oh, shut up!' says Monsieur Makossa.

'It's true though. You know how to swim?' she asks me.

'No, m'am.'

'You ought to come to the pool with me. I'll teach you how.'

'Eh, go easy, there!' yells Monsieur Makossa. 'This kid knows nothing. You shouldn't be teaching him any vices.'

'What's eating him?' she asks as she looks at me.

Then she kisses me on the forehead and says to me:

'Meet me here, Saturday at ten.'

She begins to dance, but there's no music. She stamps her feet and claps her hands as she twists and shakes to the beat. She turns her back to me and it's easy to see that she's not wearing anything under those little red shorts of hers. Monsieur Kaba goes on talking about sin and doesn't notice a thing. Monsieur Guillaume and Monsieur Laforêt steal a quick glance out of the corner of their eyes. As she keeps on dancing, she turns back around to me, but she doesn't seem to see me. All of a sudden she pivots and is back on the other side and you can tell she's humming a song.

She has a really nice voice.

'May I come along with you to the pool?' Monsieur Guillaume asks.

'Hands off, you old lecher!' she replies.

Once again she turns around. And suddenly she starts to touch her breasts, just like that. Monsieur Laforêt really seems to appreciate dance. It's wonderful! He's leaning so far forward that he's about to fall flat on his face any moment. His eyes are as big as bowling balls, he doesn't even realise he's not drinking from his glass and that all the wine is dripping on the table. And then Monsieur Kaba notices the faces on the guys in the room. He turns around and sees Mademoiselle Esther dancing.

He jumps up and knocks his glass over. His eyes are like ice. He claps his hands together once, very loudly.

'Hey, Esther!'

She's startled and turns around as if she just woke up.

Monsieur Kaba gives her an evil look.

'Oh!' she goes.

Then she quietly sits back down next to him.

'Poor little thing,' says Monsieur Guillaume. 'You can tell she's a good dancer. She could have made a really great dancer.'

◆

It really did a lot for me to have been invited to the pool by Mademoiselle Esther. I like her. You can tell right away she's a really sweet person, someone who isn't always trying to mess with you like some others I know, and then, too, I feel badly for her because without a husband, well, a woman is nothing at all. And I'd really like to see her dance professionally.

At home, I told the women right off that I was invited to the pool on Saturday. They made one of those faces! But they didn't say a thing so as not to irritate me, since I was irritated enough already. All day long I refused to eat, because I couldn't swallow anything.

'I made you a chestnut pancake,' M'am says to me.

26

'Don't want any.'

'Are you sick?'

'No.'

'What's wrong?' she asks me as she takes my hand.

'Let go of me,' I tell her. 'What do you mean what's wrong? I need a mother, that's what.'

She puts her arms around me, they're soft and their blackness shines in the light of the lamp.

I begin to cry. And I cry and cry and can't stop any more. It comes out all at once. How it hurt when I heard it. How it burnt me, too, while I was running down the street. How I don't dare look them in the face again after that.

'Don't cry, little one. There, there . . . easy now . . . Don't cry.'

And she begins to kiss the tears that are streaming down my face. After a moment I ask her:

'What's with her, my mum?'

'Don't know. She might even be dead. All I know is that your father brought you home. You were so beautiful! So cute! All blackish and shiny like charcoal. Honestly!'

She smiled.

'You know, Loukoum, I love you.'

She kisses me on the mouth.

'Mmmmmm,' she goes as if at a nice surprise.

And she says:

'Why do people have to eat all the time?'

'Well, 'cause they're hungry,' I answer.

She shakes her head as if she doesn't believe it and says:

'Maybe.'

She gets up to start dinner.

◆

My dad came back from work. He didn't say hello to anyone and sat down. He bit into a colanut. He chewed. He spat it out, far away, *splat*. He turned towards the women. He said:

'This has got to be washed, that ironed. Find me this, get me that.'

He's griping about a missing button on the shirt he put on this

27

morning. The women never stop ironing, darning his socks, finding his handkerchief.

'What's the matter?' M'am finally asks him.

'What do you mean? What should be the matter?' he asks in an angry tone of voice. 'I don't want to look like a bum, that's what's the matter. Any other wife wouldn't complain about it.'

'I'm happy about it,' she tells him.

'About what?'

'That you're well dressed. It makes me proud.'

'You really think I look OK then?'

'As if you didn't know, you rogue.'

Then he left to wash. He shaved very closely. He put on after-shave and went out.

'There's got to be a new woman,' Soumana says.

'Yeah,' M'am agreed.

'D'you know anything about it?'

'I've got my ideas.'

In the shadow of my anguish, I embrace endless glances.

I collide with the contempt of my dreams, of our dreams.

I'm looking for my face in that other place which expels me, vomits me out.

And from memories to futures, I defile my steps.

Broken hopes.

Yes, I came from far away.

I've immigrated. I've crossed frontiers. I've left fingerprints behind and, on every occasion, a shred of flesh, a bit of my soul. Yes, friend, You, you who meet me every morning and cross your everyday words with my barren syllables – you who turn your head when my eyes stare at you and come with a thousand little questions to put on your forehead – you who look away when my lips struggle, mumbling words whose foreignness dismantles your weariness and fills you with a thousand spangles – you, over there, who seem affected by nothing – you, too, you who annihilate me with your silence and beat me up whenever the desire takes you, listen:

I came to your country to guarantee myself a safe and natural death for only the dead can save their skin. I didn't know your country but I carried it on the tip of my heart. I came to work and I left my body, my blood behind, and a piece of my legends. For work devours life. My country, your forebears know it very well. They ripped out its flowers, cut down its forests, ploughed its land to strip it of the red gold of its life. I'm not resentful of them, for I have no body left, no rancour. I am lost. Withered. For once, just leave me alone – renounce your spirit of conquest, of domination, of pleasure. Just for once. Take off your purple toga, keep your hands bare, and listen with your mouth shut:

I am a man and God has created me in his image.

29

And if he, the almighty himself, carried out the parting of the waters, the division of his people into twelve tribes so as to guarantee its durability, then I, his son, faithful to his will, faithful to his spirit, I ensure my descendancy by betting on several women in order to be certain that at the end of time, when the hour of death sounds, I shall have a descendant.

Therein lies the explanation as to why every man needs to be polygamous.

(Abdou Traoré)

The following morning, Mademoiselle Garnier said:

'Children, we're going to do something special. The world is divided into developed countries and developing countries. The industrialised nations must help the poorest ones.'

The pupils are rowdy. Mademoiselle Garnier claps her hands:

'Quiet!'

And she continued:

'I'm appealing to your generosity, your courage, your sense of solidarity. I'm going to call on some of you. The first three names I call out will stand on my right. The last three will stand on my left.'

She called out some names. I was on her left.

She explained:

'When you start school, not everyone is necessarily at the same level because of culture, religion, and social differences. So I'm going to ask those on my right to help those on my left as best they can. Pierre Pelletier, would you please teach our friend Mamadou Traoré how to read?'

'Yes, m'am,' he said.

And then a girl stood up. She is wearing a great pink bow in her dark hair. She stands very straight, like a good little schoolgirl.

Mademoiselle Garnier asks:

'What are you doing, Lolita?'

The girl doesn't answer, she slowly moves forward. She still has her hands behind her back. She stands next to the teacher's desk. She takes off her sweater, folds it and puts it on the teacher's desk.

'What's come over you?'

The girl doesn't answer.

She takes off her shoes, then her socks, and puts them on the desk as well, and me, I'm noticing she has little feet with toes as cute as my thumb that you'd like to put in your mouth.

'Stop that immediately, Lolita. Put your clothes back on right now. And sit down.'

'That's not fair, Mademoiselle.'

'What's that supposed to mean, Lolita?'

'All I'm doing is handing you my contribution to help the undeveloped countries, Mademoiselle. That's what my mum does with her organisations that send aid to poor countries.'

Mademoiselle Garnier is silent. Lolita raises her eyes, frowns, and looks at her as if Mademoiselle were pestering her. Me, I'm just waiting, waiting because I'm hoping she'll also take off her dress, without wanting to cause a scandal.

'Lolita,' Mademoiselle Garnier goes, 'the help we're asking for here is of the intellectual, not the material kind. Get dressed and sit down.'

'As you wish, Mademoiselle Garnier,' Lolita says. 'As you wish. But don't go and say later that I'm selfish, which is what always happens.'

Everybody laughed.

Pierre Pelletier has slightly reddish blond hair. He's always dressed in a way others only dream about, in expensive clothes, the kind of clothes you don't find on the boulevard de Belleville. His skin is like smooth transparent milk. His face is that of a little French boy in the time of kings and princes, with his hair all curly ... And a golden personality. Before he starts his first writing lesson, he looks at me. I'm embarrassed. I'm shabbily dressed. My cap stands up in the back because I have too much hair. I'm wearing trousers that reach only to my calves. When you're growing, there's no time.

'Where are you from in Africa?' he asks.

'Mali,' I say.

'What's Mali like?'

'Dunno.'

'You don't know your own country?' he giggles and says: 'Too much!'

'I was too small.'

'Oh,' he goes. 'When I'm big, I'm going to be a navigator, and I'll travel everywhere. I'll be like Columbus.'

'Who's that, Columbus?'

He explains that he's the one who discovered America. He went over there with big boats they call sailing ships, with different names I didn't get too well. And also that the Indians were so nice to him that he brought some of them back to his own country to serve the queen.

It's difficult to grasp all this. But I'm happy, quite happy … And sad as well. So I say:

'I'd like that, too.'

'What?'

'To become a navigator.'

'You can, you know.'

'Don't think so. Niggers aren't smart.'

'Everybody's smart, Mamadou. Mademoiselle Garnier said so and she's the teacher.'

Pierre Pelletier loves Mademoiselle Garnier. There's nobody like her in the world.

◆

Saturday morning, I got up very early since I'd been invited to the swimming pool. I didn't want to eat. M'am had made an omelette and I hate them. My dad asked me:

'Who are you going to the pool with, Loukoum?'

'With Mademoiselle Esther. She invited me.'

'Don't know her.'

'She's Uncle Kaba's new woman,' I answer.

He looked at me with eyes as large as manioc balls. He stood up suddenly and so roughly that the chair fell over backwards. He put on his coat and said:

'Can't let you go off with someone I don't know. You have to show me who she is.'

'Yeah,' says M'am in a strange way.

But he isn't listening to her. Which is normal since men never listen to women, anyway …

He goes to the toilet to pee.

M'am and Soumana look at each other.

'I have to catch my breath . . .' Soumana says.

'That's right, take a deep breath, then things will be better.'

'One day I'll have to do him in; otherwise I'll have to kill myself. You don't have a recipe by any chance?'

'Like what? Plants that shred the intestines?'

'For instance.'

'Wouldn't be any good. He'd be capable of rising again like Christ, three days later, and of coming back just to give you a hard time.'

'Got to kill him.'

'Seems to me that's the worst idea you've ever had. I tell you, it serves no purpose. Besides, it's a sin; that's what's written in the Koran.'

'I can't stand it any more.'

'Don't worry. He comes and goes. You haven't got used to it as far as I can see. You'd better get used to it or else you'll go under.'

'It's hard being a woman, you know.'

'It's not any easier to be preaching in the desert like Mohammed,' she says.

You can hear the pee flowing noisily.

'But really, at this rate I'm going to fall apart.'

'Seems to me it's too much of a thrill for men when women fall apart on account of them. On the contrary, you should live.'

'How do you do that?'

'Sou, what would you say if you were in my place?'

Soumana didn't say another word. You'd think someone had cut her off just like that, cut the voice right inside her throat. Her face is very sad, flustered.

'I've loved Abdou from the very first day I saw him. I swear to you, M'am! But when I see him carry on, I feel like slitting his throat from one end to the other.'

She pants a little and adds:

'In the end, you are the one who deserves more pity.'

'That's normal. I am the legitimate one and I'm the one he's dragging through the mud.'

'And yet you don't say anything. You're like all the women back home, like my mother, my grandmother, and her mother before that.

Always at the feet of the men, saying thank you, that's fine, bravo to everything they wreck on earth. My father, he never even paid any attention to us, as if Mum had brought us into the world by herself!'

'How many kids did she have, your mother?'

'Dunno. The wives, there were thirty of them. And each one must have given birth six times at least. You figure it out.'

'And how were they together?'

'They worked in the fields and then, to get that out of their minds, they would fight with each other all the time and bully each other's children just to get back at my dad. Me, I used to think they should have united against him and beat him up until they killed him. But instead they allowed him to reign over them like a lord. Little did I know then I would be living the same dog's life.'

'*Inch Allah!*' M'am says.

'That's all you can say. But tell me, M'am, how do you manage to stand having Abdou around?'

'It's the survival instinct,' says M'am. 'It gives you strength which you draw from inside, deep in your gut. And anyway for me it's so deep down now, my hatred, it doesn't even surface any more ... Except for the *gloo-gloc*, of course!'

They burst out laughing. We hear the toilet being flushed.

'How about mending the children's socks?' M'am suggests.

And off they go to get what they need.

34

Fortune! What a farce!

I've waited for the promised healing.

I've touched what lies in the heart that cannot be spoken.

My soul has cracked to the point of howling and I weep over the hours that have been torn apart.

So, you'll say to me, and why? Why woman, women, why am I here on this earth, this fragile horizon of huddled dreams? Don't ask any more, don't ask. Exile has emptied my memory and admires its drowning. But, there is woman. She is there, vast, inaccessible, present and so distant. She comes in, an ocean in flames, puts her lips on my unconscious soul. She pushes that door, on the left side of my chest. I placed a few diamonds there, when I was still in Africa, and I lost the keys.

She lays her clothes on the fingers of the stars. Her body leans over, she takes my hand. 'You are the pearl, the human pearl. Who sends you? God or the devil? No. Don't answer me. Let me be. Let me reinforce that tower you wanted to construct and which exile is crucifying – And this little nest? You wanted to build it? Don't say anything. I read it in your body. Don't be afraid any more. I shall build the nest of your dreams' shores for you.'

A heavy sob sits on the edge of my eye. I clasp on to her breast, her belly, the warm fleece of her sex, as if on to a new land, a new dawn. And for me these images reinvent the legends of before in a mystical farandole.

Exile serves as a truce.

(Abdou Traoré)

35

We arrived at the café. You wouldn't believe how busy it was. My dad says hello to Monsieur Kaba.

Monsieur Kaba asks:

'And, my dear Abdou, what's new?'

'Oh, not much. Everyone's fine, *inch Allah*.'

'And the wife?'

'Fine, fine.'

'I suppose she can't even go for a walk from what I can tell. Always working. It would be nice if my wives followed her example. It would save me money.'

Monsieur Kaba is always talking about money, as if he were broke. But he's got so much he doesn't know what to do with it. It's my dad who's the poorest in this crowd, after Monsieur Laforêt that is!

'So where is she? Where is the loveliest of them all?' asks my dad. 'I have something for her.'

He takes a bar of chocolate out of his pocket and puts it on the table.

'In the bathroom,' answers Monsieur Kaba. 'She's had such a rough night . . .'

'And what about you, Guillaume, how are things?' my dad asks.

And he bites into a colanut with gusto. Then, making a lot of noise, he chews. And goes on:

'Seems Esther wants to take the boy to the pool.'

'Yeah,' goes Monsieur Guillaume. 'That child is a real womaniser.'

My father strokes his bald head.

'She's a bit of all right, that woman!'

'Costly, too, a chick like that!' says Monsieur Guillaume.

I see my dad suddenly jump up and he says:

'Esther!'

Yes, it's Mademoiselle Esther. She's wearing black tights with a leotard under her coat. With her hair divided into two braids, she looks like a child. My dad looks at her. His eyes are devouring her face.

'Well, well, that's a surprise!' she says.

Everyone is looking at her. When she reaches us, Monsieur Kaba pulls up a chair. But she doesn't sit down. She picks up the chocolate bar.

'Such treats! You want a piece?' she asks me.

I say no. Then she pouts like a little girl and bites into it, huh!

'It's delicious. But I should watch my weight.'

'You're perfect as you are.'

'You think everything I do is perfect. But that's because you don't know what's what.'

She starts to laugh. My dad looks crestfallen.

◆

We went to the swimming pool. I don't have any swimming trunks. I've kept my underpants on. They're completely black with a little turd in the bottom because I don't wipe my behind too carefully. Mademoiselle Esther has taken her coat off. She's as thin as a rake with a waist the size of my fist. She has breasts like I've never seen before, with tips on which you'd like to put your mouth. I've never seen anything prettier.

Suddenly she stops dead in her tracks as she notices what I'm looking at. She makes big eyes at me.

'What are you looking at me like that for?' she asks. 'You wouldn't be a midget by any chance? How old are you, anyway?'

'Ten.'

'Oh Lord! Oh no! These niggers!'

But I just go on looking.

'You a virgin?' she asks me.

'Yeah,' I go.

'Your mother never showed you her breasts?'

'Can't remember that she did,' I answer. 'But I've seen Soumana a few times. She doesn't count, though. She's nothing but fat everywhere, if you know what I mean.'

'Well then, make the most of it!'

And then she turns around, turns again, shows her titties, her behind, all pink with spots on it like freckles. She rolls her eyes upward and I feel my hands trembling and my heart racing inside my chest. Suddenly she throws me a strange look.

'Stop!' she says. 'That's enough!'

'As you say, Miss,' I answer.

37

Mademoiselle Esther has put my clothes in a locker which she shut with a snap! She attached the key of the locker to my wrist with a blue bracelet that looks like a watch. And the thought occurred to me that I'd really like to have a watch. Then we went to the pool. It's like the sea, only it's in a basin and it doesn't reach the Americas as I wish it would. She put a lifejacket on me: 'So you won't drown,' she told me with a big laugh. But I was wet through and through on the inside, that's how afraid I was of the water. I was trembling.

'Do you think I can stand there on the edge?' I ask her. 'I don't know how to swim.'

'Oh! there's no danger. And anyway I'm here.'

Finally we get into the water together, very slowly, to see how deep it is. Since she didn't bring a bathing cap, she puts up her hair and fastens it with a hairpin. She swims across the pool and back to show me what you do with your arms and legs. After that she holds me flat on my belly on the water so I can practise.

After a short while, I begin to get the hang of it. I swim a few yards before sinking when she lets go of me. I shriek. I'm scared.

'The important thing is not to be afraid,' she tells me. 'Water won't hurt you.'

Then she swims several laps across the pool. Just for fun. I don't dare move. There are several children in the water. They're jumping around, they're splashing, and they never stop screaming.

Finally we get out of the water and go back to the dressing room. She shakes out her hair to let it dry. Now it's like crushed corn and glued to her neck and face. She's awfully pretty.

'Did you like that?' she asks.

'Yeah,' I say.

'Good for you, you have to know how to enjoy the good things in life.'

'Yeah. It's really very nice of you to teach me how to swim. My dad always told me that one day he'd take me to the pool, but he never has time. Do you think we can come back again?'

'Of course! Why not? With all those guys sticking their thing up you, a little exercise and some fresh air won't do me any harm.'

I didn't really understand what she meant, but in any case it doesn't make any difference considering I think she's splendid, and if you have the luck to have a girl of that calibre teach you how to swim, so much the better for you.

'Shall we go?' she asks.

◆

We had pizza in a bar. Mademoiselle Esther eats like a bird. So I ate both slices, and washed it down with a soda.

Then we went to the park at the Buttes-Chaumont. It's like a zoo, only there are trees and forests. It was chilly again as it always is when Christmas is close. As soon as we walked into the park, I inhaled the air. It was as if we were somewhere else. Really, another country. Because in there the air was light, light as a feather, that's why I breathed deeply to give myself a dose of good health. Everything around us was green. Of course there were some dead leaves on the ground. They were brown, because there was still a bit of autumn. The flowers smelt good along the paths that twisted and turned in and around themselves so that you could get lost without anyone able to find you. Birds were singing their heads off in the trees. Pigeons were taking flight in a flurry of feathers when we came close; all this was very different from Paris, from everything I'd known until then. Even the sun, you'd have thought this was the place it was born and would go to sleep.

'How pretty! I didn't know there were bits of heaven right here in Paris,' I said.

'Yeah. But nobody has time to come here. Everybody is always too busy in this country.'

We go up a footbridge. On the other side we end up in front of a pink chalet, a restaurant for the rich people of Paris's sixteenth *arrondissement*. Further on, there is a waterfall and from where we stand you'd say these were the tears of the sun.

'Have you done any natural science at school?' Mademoiselle Esther asks me.

'A little,' I answer. 'But I didn't learn all the names of trees, flowers, birds, and all that.'

'That is a willow. This one is a plum tree. And the other one, over there, is called a pine tree. Can you remember those names?'

'I'll do what I can, Mademoiselle,' I answer. 'But what's for sure is that it's very beautiful! And so quiet!'

'That's only normal. Today is Saturday and everyone is shopping.'

As soon as she stops talking, my eyes catch sight of a hat. It is my father's. Anyway, he is making big motions with his hand to attract our kind attention.

Dad is dressed to outshine even the sun. He's wearing a candy-pink jacket and a wide-brimmed beige hat with a dip in the middle, like a stetson. He is balancing on his feet like a schoolboy who wants to be noticed, and everyone does take notice.

'Hi! Didn't keep you waiting, I hope?'

'Hi,' Mademoiselle Esther answers, speechless with surprise.

Me, I'm surprised too, but I say nothing. I'm wondering where he could possibly have found the money to dress so elegantly, which is not exactly in line with our level of family expenditure. My dad, the very one here before me, is not the same any more. I swear, you wouldn't think this is a guy who works for the Sanitation Department to keep Paris clean. I look at him, eyes wide with astonishment. He pays no attention to me because he is too busy wooing Mademoiselle Esther. Got to understand and forgive when you can.

'We had a good time at the pool,' Mademoiselle Esther goes. 'Loukoum has a real knack for it.'

'Yeah,' goes my dad. 'Do you want something to drink?'

'I'm not thirsty,' she answers.

Then we began to walk.

My dad took Mademoiselle Esther's hand. They walk hand in hand because they want to be friends. He talks, she giggles. He says dumb things, she giggles. She giggles at no matter what bullshit he delivers and she throws her head back, shows her neck and what's inside her blouse.

'You're very lovely, Esther.'

'Thank you.'

'You've got a lovely pair, splendid thighs, and your rump, well, it's hot.'

'Thank you.'

'Maybe you don't need me to tell you that with all the many men who surround you . . .'

40

'It's always a pleasure for a girl to hear a man compliment her. It's never too much.'

She bursts out laughing.

True, we are still in the park of the Buttes-Chaumont, the most beautiful place in the land, but I no longer see it. The birds are singing, I no longer hear them. There's like a ball in my gullet. If this continues, I think I'm going to strangle my dad. But there you have it, the Koran forbids that, it says so in black and white: 'Thou shalt honour thy father, thy mother, whatever happens . . .'

'I have to leave you,' my dad says.

'There you go,' I murmur between my teeth.

'What did you say, Loukoum?' my dad asks.

'Just that I'm sorry you've got to go so soon,' I lie.

'Oh, my son, oh my son,' he goes, all happy.

Then he kisses Mademoiselle Esther sweetly on both cheeks. She turns her head to watch him go up the path and signals him with her hand. Then she turns to me. First she smiles. Then she bends over so her face is right at the level of mine and says: 'You, you're very handsome too, and elegant and everything.'

She ruffles my hair. Then she remains thoughtful for a few moments and says:

'I wonder how anyone can put up with your father. His wives, how do they manage?'

'You manage to put up with him quite well, Mademoiselle Esther,' I retort. 'How do you do it?'

'Only the good Lord knows.'

And she bursts out laughing.

'You've got to have a good time every now and then. And for a good time with a guy, there's nothing better than a nigger.'

◆

It was already dark when we got back to the café. There weren't many people there any more, just Monsieur Guillaume and a few people I didn't know. So I went home. M'am and Soumana were in the kitchen. Soumana was slicing plantains and M'am was frying them. I took a few to have something to eat and Soumana asked if we'd gone

41

swimming. I answered that we had and told them that Mademoiselle Esther had terrific breasts, and that we'd taken a walk in the park with my dad. They looked at each other and Soumana made a wrong move and cut her finger.

'No, really . . .' Soumana goes.

'I'll be damned,' M'am says. 'Do you realise what that means?'

'That's what I was doing actually.'

And she goes off to bandage her finger.

When she came back, M'am had finished cooking the plantains and they put them on the table.

'I'm not hungry,' says Soumana.

'You'd better eat something,' M'am goes.

'Not as long as . . .'

At that point she knits her thick eyebrows, then says:

'Why does the good Lord hate women?'

'He loves us but he doesn't want to show it, that's why,' M'am says.

'What arseholes!'

'Who?'

'The good Lord! Men! Life! They all stink.'

'You don't really believe that, Sou!'

'Oh no? That so-and-so would do well not to cross my path or else I'll break his fat face.'

'What's the most shocking to you? That Abdou cheats on you or that the good Lord watches without reacting?'

'Both,' she retorts.

'If it makes you feel any better, Abdou had other women when we were going together. He'd disappear for days and nights on end. One day he came back, put me on his lap just like that and said: "Forgive me".'

'I don't believe you.'

'I'm telling you, you ought to believe me. He was quite a lady-killer at the time, he used to run after anything in a skirt. But he'd always come back, d'you get it?'

'Yeah, but I won't accept it.'

'You'd better accept the reality.'

'No. He's going to have to choose. Me or that slut.'

M'am shakes her head sadly.

'Sou, it's a painful choice that you're going to force him to make. We'll miss you, you know.'

'He wouldn't dare!'

'Yes, he would. Maybe we're just too old or too ugly for him.'

'No! No, no, and no again!' Soumana shrieks.

She's screaming so loudly that she can be heard for miles and her howling wakes Fatima, my sister. Fatima is a ballbreaker of the first order. She pesters for two and acts more stupidly than twelve hundred could. And always something or other in her little snout; always nibbling, always bawling.

'What's happening?' she asks. 'Why are you screaming?'

'Because God refuses to hear me, my girl.'

'That's no reason to disturb the sleep of honest citizens,' she replies. 'Can I have some sweets, Mummy?'

Soumana says yes.

'There's God's gift to you,' M'am says, pointing at Fatima.

A land with a flayed body. Mine.

I am the despair of a poor people, deprived, forgotten by the gods, banished by men.

The old men clutch on to bits of dried-up land.

The old women pray.

The young believe in it.

They speak of revolution. Their hands are bare. They have no weapons.

They want death.

They challenge it.

Why do you want to die?

'I have sinned. I must be punished.'

Punish? But punish whom? And for what? For being free to love the bitter cola, palm wine and the woman in love, for preferring day to night, the stars to the disciplines, to the macerations of sadness.

I come from a land planted with forests, with sun and clay. My parents used to live there. Men arrived. The trees disappeared. Bodies closed over wounds. Never named. Vanquished, pride stooped down. My memory was emptied. Who am I? Dust? Illusion? Tell me, friend. Yes, friend. My parents are no longer there to remind me that I am the dawn of a secret. An unfinished story. Tell me, friend. For friendship settles many a pending question. Speak to me of myself. Tell me of the throng. They say that it is bowing down, kneeling down, and causing night to fall over its memories. It is poor. I know that. And mute as well. Its mouth rotten from the sins the leaders invent. Is that true, friend?

(Abdou Traoré)

At school, Pierre Pelletier teaches me how to read and write. It's cool but it's hard. He teaches me how to write words and a lot of things he thinks I should know. He doesn't let go of me. To that end he is quite single-minded. He is a good schoolteacher. He is really wicked that kid. He makes me read. He writes things in his beautiful handwriting. The problem is that I have trouble cramming everything he explains to me into my head. But Pierre Pelletier's other name is patience. So he explains. He really is stubborn, that guy.

'You've got to struggle,' he repeats to me endlessly. 'You must! You must!'

I find that kind of terrain rather slippery. I just want to save my hide.

When Pierre Pelletier is teaching me, all the girls come over as soon as they can. Especially Lolita. She asks me, 'So, how's it going?' But I'm not blind. I can see clearly that she's crazy about him. Sometimes she puts on her Sunday best and escapes for good when Pierre is reading me a dictation or tries to fill my head with lots of new things. He looks somewhere else as if he didn't see her. If I were in his place . . . But nothing is in its place, so . . .

Mademoiselle Garnier said that I was making progress.

I made a bracelet for Lolita. I took some old sandals of my dad's that I cut up to get the leather. I polished the strips really well, I dyed them with clay, dried them, and then braided them together. In fact, I've never made anything for anyone, except for Allah when I go to the mosque. So anyway, I don't really dare show Lolita my bracelet in case she should make fun of me. Sometimes I see Lolita in the courtyard. She's with her friend. She's dressed like a princess with her blue woollen dress and matching tights. She always has a big bow in her hair. She's so elegant! I believe that all the birds in the sky sing just for her alone. Then I feel my heart turning over. 'Come here! come here!' I'd like to cry out to her, with Allah's help, that would really contribute something to my life. But I say nothing, seeing that I don't really belong here and that she also hasn't asked me anything. Sometimes she thinks that I don't see her and she throws me odd looks as if I were a strange animal. Then she bursts out laughing. Her friends too.

But me, I just keep my head up high. And then I study with Pierre

Pelletier. I draw the letters *a*, and *o*, and *c*. Soon I'm putting the letters together to make TO EAT TO SLEEP TO GO OUT.

'Soon you'll be a whiz, my friend,' Pierre Pelletier goes to me.

One day, I get brave and I show Lolita the bracelet.

'How pretty!' she says. 'Where did you get it?'

'I made it myself. It's for you.'

'Really?'

'Yeah.'

She puts the bracelet on.

'Oh! Mamadou, you're a real genius.'

Me, I just lower my head.

She runs down the playground and shows it to everyone. She is laughing. In any case, she is magnificent. She shows Pierre and Johanne how pretty the bracelet is.

'Can you make me one?' Johanne asks.

'Of course,' I answer.

'And then you could make one for Pierre, too,' says Lolita. 'That would be a nice way to thank him and to show him your work.'

What a brilliant idea. At home, I cut up an old pair of snakeskin sandals, all the while thinking about the kind of bracelet Pierre Pelletier might like. He is nice, he is handsome, and he doesn't talk much. He supports me in everything I want to do and when he touches me, you'd think that his hands know what I want. So I start his bracelet. It will have to be wider than Lolita's, soft, comfortable . . .

So I cut it, I braid it and I finish it. And then I give it to him.

The first piece of news after this is that Johanne now really wants one, too, and Lolita wants one just like Pierre Pelletier's and all the guys in the class want one. In no time at all, I'm snowed under. I'm really wondering where I might find other old pairs of sandals.

'You should sell your bracelets,' Pierre says to me.

'How?'

'Well, you suggest a price . . .'

Then he thinks it over for a moment and says:

'Three francs a bracelet. Whoever wants one just has to pay up. That's it, pal, you're on your way.'

In the days that followed I worked like a madman. I was learning to read and write. I was really applying myself since Pierre Pelletier

wouldn't stop telling me that I had to if I wanted to be smart. I was
making bracelets. On Saturdays I went swimming with Mademoiselle
Esther. Now I know how to swim and Mademoiselle Esther is very
proud of that and doesn't stop complimenting me.

It was on our way back from the swimming pool that there was a
scandal at Monsieur Guillaume's café. My dad was there, and Monsieur Kaba, Monsieur Laforêt, Monsieur Ndongala, my uncle Kouam
who married a white woman who wears trousers even though she is
old, and a whole tribe of niggers who can't all be described seeing as
there were so many of them. Everybody was drinking and toasting and
cracking the usual jokes. I can't explain all of it to you, but I swear to
you there's nothing like getting black folks together to see how much
noise can be made. They laugh about absolutely nothing at all. They
clap their hands, their thighs, throw their heads back and laugh with
their teeth showing like chicks who are waiting to be fondled.
Sometimes they sing. They sing quite out of tune but that really isn't
important. It was at that moment that Monsieur Guillaume took the
thing out. A little man of straw with a white face and lots of needles
stuck everywhere in its body.

'Oh!' Monsieur Kaba screamed.

'Fantastic!' Mademoiselle Esther said.

'What's that?' my dad asked.

'A fetish, of course!' Monsieur Guillaume answered.

'A fetish?' they all exclaimed.

'Yeah!' Monsieur Guillaume went.

'Oh!!!' they all went, rolling their eyes as if they'd just seen a
monster.

Then my dad closed his eyes and recited incantations to chase the
demons away. Afterwards he said:

'That's evil!'

'Why, dad?' I asked.

'It's a sin.'

'But you have one, too.'

He didn't answer me. He pointed his finger at the fetish and said:

'Evil! Evil!'

'Yeah,' my uncle Kouam went. 'It's the incarnation of the devil.'

Then Monsieur Kaba got into it, too. His face was completely dark.

47

'Armageddon!' he was shouting. 'Jezebel! Cain! It's the destruction of the just in the boiling waters of hell! I told you so! I warned you!'

Monsieur Guillaume was very much impressed. You could see it in his eyes, completely surprised, and staring with a look asking why. It was the first time he'd ever seen black people as excited as a thousand sailboats adrift.

'I think it's rather cute,' he stuttered.

'Me too,' said Mademoiselle Esther. 'He is funny with his white hat and black suit.'

And at that point she burst out laughing. Her laugh is like the water of a fountain. Clear. Limpid.

All the blacks turned towards her. A thousand pairs of eyes were staring at her.

'All right, guys, I'm not your devil, you know! Anyway, all that is ignorance, superstition, and nothing more!'

Monsieur Kaba's face turned purple with indignation; he filled his glass with a trembling hand pouring some wine on the oilcloth. Spilling wine from a glass brings bad luck. You then have to ward off fate by spitting on the ground three times. My father took that task upon himself.

Monsieur Kaba drank a sip of wine. He put his glass down. Then he sniggered nastily.

'Just take a look at that girl, will you, calling a man ignorant. She knows nothing about anything.'

It took Mademoiselle Esther's breath away. She lit a cigarette without a word.

'I left school in the sixth grade,' he started again in a hoarse voice. 'But you, with your white education, your *lycée*, the *bac* and all that, and you're still a kid. Frankly, you still have an awful lot to learn.'

'I wasn't born yesterday, you know!' Mademoiselle Esther replied. 'I know a lot more than you might imagine.'

Me, too, I knew things.

From my earliest childhood on, I'd learned a lot of things as part of this tribe, all sorts of precious traditions that come down from one generation to the next since our earliest ancestors, the Touaregs. But sometimes I forget. For example, I have known for many years that to avoid the evil eye, you must wear a golden chain, for the sorcerer who

48

attacks you is distracted by gold, he begins to try schemes to rip it away from you and then leaves you alone. I know that the first urine in the morning is a pure miracle for getting rid of pimples, but until now I haven't had the opportunity to use that panacea. And of course I know that a crushed stone heals angina and a red shell gets rid of the measles. Every time I have a fever, M'am ties a clove of garlic to my wrist and each time the fever goes down. I know that if you sleep with the windows open, all the neighbouring sorcerers will come into the house, so you should put a glass of water on the windowsill: the sorcerers will drown. I also know that putting a knife in the rain will keep lightning away from the house. I know all that. But Monsieur Kaba is right: you can never be smart enough.

The laughter was over. My dad pushed his chair away and put on his overcoat.

'Let's go, son.'

It was like a signal. All the blacks left the café, in single file, without another word.

Outside, cool air filled the immense, powerful, and infinite sky. My dad took out a cigarette and lit it.

'Why is Monsieur Guillaume's fetish so bad?' I asked my dad again.

'Because in our religion it is forbidden to have a representation of the human face.'

'Tell me, Dad, why do you have one then?'

'It's not the same thing,' he answered.

But I personally don't see the difference.

The business of Monsieur Guillaume's fetish so profoundly touched the blacks that measures had to be taken. Monsieur Guillaume is well liked by the blacks, seeing that he has adopted a white child who is really black. Suddenly, because of a fetish, every black in Belleville couldn't stand him any longer. He was accused of everything, from having dirty hands, feet that smell, serving beer watered down with dishwater, cheating his customers, shacking up with fascists, all the way to practising human sacrifices. Nobody went there any more, except for Monsieur Laforêt.

This must have lasted a good two weeks, Monsieur Guillaume's difficulties. Then one morning, without any further developments, everybody changed their minds, it seemed the blacks were just tired of finding him so nasty. It was Monsieur Kaba who led the way.

'So, old man, how're things?' he asked Monsieur Guillaume with an enormous smile.

'Fine,' he answered.

'Long time no see, eh?'

'Yeah.'

So the whole tribe returned in single file. Monsieur Guillaume received them as if nothing had happened. The old customs were taken up again. The blacks gave him *salaam aleikoum* and smiled, slapping him on the shoulder as if they'd left the evening before.

Me, I was completely astounded. I didn't understand a thing. With niggers, you shouldn't try to understand.

I lost my soul over an ocean.

I am a scrap of difference that makes fools angry.

My steps in the streets raise the barrier walls higher and reinforce the stones of indifference.

I am the immigrant, the exiled star, and I go forward with my head turned back.

I try not to weigh too much, to be a crumpled piece of paper, just in case some angels should come to carry me off to heaven, close to the Lord.

I am a noise, barely a breath.

And yet, the old hag flees before me, her bag clutched under her armpits.

Further along, in the parts of the city where the houses are made of stone and where they don't want to hear the cries of suffering, a few roaming dogs and cats fling themselves at my heels.

I am transparent.

A word difficult to pronounce.

An illness one catches.

But you, friend, listen without passing judgment, let me live close to the world, the lifetime of a star, for yet another quarter of the moon, and listen:

In this room as wide as a coffin – MY HOUSE.

I sing of the joy of being loved while I regret a thousand times what is inaccessible to me.

I delude my eyes with tenderness, isolated from mankind and from time which showers my life with shame and blood.

I am melting into a trembling willow,

cowering in the deepest corners of unconfessed dreams,

That beg my soul for oblivion.

(Abdou Traoré)

I sleep, I wake up. I sleep, I wake up again, I fall asleep again, and wake up once more. It really is true, I just can't manage to sleep. I work all day long. I read. I swim. I make bracelets. But I can't manage to fall asleep. I try the trick of counting sheep and it doesn't work either. I make Superman come to me. Superman is the dog I made up in my head when M'am said that 'when people have nothing to eat, there's nothing to fill up a dog either'. So Superman licks my face with his tongue but for God's sake that doesn't work either. So I stay awake until M'am says: 'Light costs money'. So I turn it off. But I still can't sleep. Maybe I did something wrong and the good Lord is punishing me. Then I think: yeah, I did hurt M'am's feelings.

◆

I get up. It's awfully quiet. So quiet you can hear yourself breathe. Personally I rather like that; it's a change from the noises of Paris in the daytime. In the street there's a dog walking all by himself, his nose to the ground.

'What's the matter? Why aren't you asleep?' M'am asks.

'Don't feel like it.'

'Are you sick?'

I tell her no. She frowns, then says: 'When a man can't sleep he's got something on his conscience.'

'Yeah.'

'Mmmmm, I see.'

I see it in her eyes, that she sees, that she's already seen it all, and that she's plagued by the same things and that she, too, thinks a lot.

'I'm really ashamed, M'am. I thought bad things of you and of other people, too, because you are not my mum.'

'I'm not happy about that by any means, Loukoum.'

'Where is my mother?'

'I've no idea. I've never even seen her.'

'And you never heard from her?'

'No.'

'She must be dead.'

'Why don't you talk to your father,' she advises me. 'After all, he is your father. There has to be something he can tell you about it.'

'I love you, M'am.'

She smiled, then lifted her hands to her face.

◆

Dad and I talked for hours. I wanted to know what she's like, my mum, tall or short? What sort of clothes does she wear? Does she know how to read? Can she cook well? And her skin? And her hair?

I really wanted to know everything about my mum. Dad talks and talks until he has no voice left.

'Why do you want to know so much about your mother?'

'Because she is my mother, even if she doesn't love me.'

◆

After that we went to the mosque. We put on our white *djellabas*, both the same, and our matching mosque *chechias*, except that the knot in the back of his is red and mine yellow. We went down the rue Jean-Pierre-Timbaud. It's a bit chilly but the sun is shining. We're very chic. We're walking side by side. As we're going to the mosque, he explains a lot of things to me. We are really making a good impression. Women turn around and smile at him. M'am and Soumana are staying home – Muslim women don't go inside the mosque because of impurity or something like that, which I haven't really understood.

After the service, father exchanged tons of *salaam aleikoums* with other Muslims. There are Arabs who are Muslim too. But it isn't the same.

Then we went to Monsieur Guillaume's café. The whole black tribe is there. They drink a bit and they talk.

My aunt Mathilda is there with my uncle Kouam. My aunt Mathilda wears trousers or skirts that are too short, she drinks cognac, and she smokes. Sometimes when my father talks about her, he uses words like 'whore', 'slut', 'floozy', and 'tart'. But he never says anything when my aunt Mathilda's there. He even smiles at her.

'So, my girl, how are things?'

'I'm worn out,' she goes.

Besides her cute arse, which she wriggles on her fancy high heels, my aunt has a pretty face. She tells me good stories. But dad says that she doesn't behave like a Muslim's honourable wife should.

My uncle Kouam is a civil servant somewhere. He's playing the horses. First he bets on 3, Joli-Coeur, then on 7, then on 9, Paradise.

'You've got to be the king of morons to put a single cent on that one,' Monsieur Guillaume says. 'Even if Zorro rode him, he's sure to finish in the pasture.'

'He'd do well to stop playing,' says my aunt Mathilda.

Then she goes on to explain that it's time for her to get a new car because the one they have nobody would want, not even as a gift. Then she goes to the door, glances at the car and says:

'A pile of scrap iron.'

'What she needs is a kid,' my father says to my uncle Kouam.

'She doesn't want any.'

'You don't need her permission. Women are only good for . . .'

But then he doesn't finish his sentence.

My uncle Kouam shakes his head and says:

'You're a lucky man, you know. That one there, I swear, she's as stubborn as a mule.'

Afterwards I ask my aunt Mathilda:

'How come you're as stubborn as a mule?'

'Who told you that?'

I don't answer.

'Why are you his wife?'

'It's fate.'

'Yeah,' I say. 'Me too, I'll meet my fate. I'm going to get married . . .'

'No kidding!'

'Yeah.'

'Who is she?'

'A girl at my school.'

She laughs and says:

'Puppy love.'

'No, it's serious.'

'And her mother, what's she have to say about it?'

'I don't know her.'

'And her father?'

'I've no idea who he is.'

'And she herself, what's she have to say?'

'I haven't told her anything.'

'Well now! And that's how you're going to get married, little man? Congratulations.'

But I can see in her face that she doesn't believe a word of it.

◆

Father has been gone for several days. He doesn't come back home and Miss Esther had disappeared as well. She no longer comes swimming with me. The women are talking among themselves. M'am prays, that's all she does, pray. And Soumana is rage itself. Sometimes she says:

'I won't calm down till I've killed him.'

The children look at her and start to cry and yell: 'Mummy! Mummy! . . .' But she doesn't seem to hear them. She pays no attention to the kids any longer. She often touches them, but not even like if you stroke a dog. It's more like she's touching a footstool or a piece of wood. It's M'am who does her woman's work. Sometimes my sisters have nightmares. They scream. That wakes everybody up. M'am turns on the light and checks them. She pats them on the shoulder and consoles them. She's really very good with us.

Today, M'am brought a woman home. A white one. She wears a camelhair coat. She's got a lot of hair on her head, very blonde, which makes her look quite extraordinary.

'Let me introduce my friend,' says M'am.

Her name is Madame Saddock. She speaks softly as if everyone was asleep, but nobody is sleeping. She looks around her with eyes like this. Perhaps she thinks that we belong to a minority, since we don't have the basic necessities such as the city gas of Paris which doesn't come all the way out here. But she makes no comments. As soon as she opened her mouth I thought right away that it was no big deal.

'It's unpardonable,' she goes. 'Intolerable. You've got to fight it! I'm not going to do it for you.'

'That's true enough,' Soumana says. 'I've had it up to here.'

'So what are you waiting for? For your life to be in a shambles? . . .'

'I can't take it any more,' she says. 'That man, he's the bad seed. He spoils everything.'

'It bothers you because you think he's everywhere all the time,' says M'am. 'You think he's God. But he isn't. Talk to your God about it. Entrust him with your life and you'll see that everything will go much better.'

'That's not so easy,' says Soumana.

'She's right,' says Madame Saddock. 'I don't even know if God exists. On the other hand, I do know that men exist, they're everywhere and you have to fight them.'

'God does exist,' says M'am. 'When a guy is a pain in the arse, think of the flowers, think of the trees. All those are God's creations. He made them for women, because men are blind to them.'

'I can't take it any more!' Soumana yells. 'God or no God, I want to live my life.'

'That's your right,' says Madame Saddock.

'Yeah. I want a life.'

'You already have something,' M'am retorts. 'You have children.'

'So does he, but that doesn't stop him from abandoning them and running after other women.'

'You could divorce,' Madame Saddock suggests.

'She'd have to be married first,' goes M'am.

'OK. So you can leave whenever you want.'

'It's not that simple,' Soumana answers.

'And why not?' asks Madame Saddock. 'You're free, you can go whenever you want!'

'And my children, what's going to become of them?'

'No problem, children are always entrusted to their mother.'

'That's what you say! I can't even state that my children are my children.'

'Why do you say that?'

''Cause I've no papers, I've nothing. The children came out of my belly and that's it. It's M'am who lent me her papers so I could go to the delivery room. So . . .'

'That's terrible,' Madame Saddock says. 'Scandalous! I can't imagine such things going on in this day and age.'

'After all, it was men who killed the son of God . . . It's not really important,' M'am goes.

At that point they looked at each other with great big eyes.

Then Madame Saddock asks:

'May I smoke?'

'Yeah,' M'am answers and goes to the window. She opens it and says:

'Be careful with the ash too, in case he comes home and notices it.'

'Don't you want one?' Madame Saddock then asks.

'Our religion forbids it,' Soumana answers.

'You should try one.'

'I don't fancy it. They seem to make you sick.'

Madame Saddock lights her cigarette. She takes a drag and says:

'Old wives' tales. My father used to smoke like a chimney and he died in his bed when he was over eighty-five years old.'

Madame Saddock began to explain a load of stuff to the women. She talked about associations in defence of women, of the '68 women's revolution in which women united their forces. From that date on, she goes, women have the same rights as men. They are free. They work. They realise their dreams. She said a whole lot more, about women who were in charge of things in offices, about women doctors, about women in politics. She talked so much that she had no voice left. I know all of this already, but I don't see that it makes any difference.

Then she asked for a piece of paper and a pencil. She scribbled something that she gave to Soumana. Then she got up and left.

◆

My dad came back after one week. He was staggering and fell in a heap into his armchair. He looked sad and totally wiped out. He said nothing to anyone. I had masses of questions on the tip of my tongue I was dying to ask: Where had he been? Who with? What happened to him? I was biting my tongue not to ask them.

After that, he slept until lunchtime. When the women finished cooking, he opened one eye.

And there he is, coming out of the bedroom, dragging his feet like an old clod. He sits down in his chair. He turns on the television. He takes out his cola nut, bites off a piece, chews, spits against the wall, *splat*! And he turns to Soumana.

'Bring me a glass of water,' he says without flinching.

She raises her eyes and looks at him.

First, her face doesn't move. Her wide, flat nose stays the same. And also her mouth, plump as a prune. Only her large eyes are glittering. They look as if they'd like to kill a snake. Then she looks my dad over from head to toe and clucks:

'At last!' she says.

Later, I grew bold and asked:

'Tell me, daddy, what exactly is that, a liberated woman?'

Without looking up, my dad goes:

'Who told you about that?'

'I dunno, I'm just talking.'

I don't dare tell him about Madame Saddock.

'Nobody listens to what those kind of women have to say. They just chatter like magpies. There's not a man around who wants anything to do with them. Which is why they're into revolutions.'

He bit into his cola nut, chewed it, and said:

'Listen, Loukoum, you're my heir. One day, all that I have will be yours. So listen carefully. That sort of woman is bad news, spreads her legs for anyone. Never listen to them. Never!'

I wouldn't want to be Soumana's heir, I promise you! An eighty-five kilo black woman, each kilo grosser than the next, that's weird.

The women have prepared couscous. It's very nutritious. Except that Fatima won't stop crying. My dad hit her.

After that, I went over my writing because tomorrow there's a spelling test.

◆

The spelling test wasn't easy. It wasn't very hard either, except that French has some complicated words and I don't write fast. By the time I was finishing the word RANGER, they were already at MANGER. It didn't make me feel very good. But I did what I could. Pierre Pelletier, on the other hand, writes with ease. When he finished, he looked over at my work and smiled at me encouragingly.

After school, Mademoiselle Garnier called me, leaned over, held out her hand to me, and said:

'Congratulations, Mamadou! You did quite well.'

She has wonderful hands, long ones with clearly defined pink nails. Looking at them is like looking at a merry-go-round.

'You should keep this up.'

'*Inch Allah*,' I say.

She laughed. She turned her back and left.

That shocked me.

I hung around for a while, mostly to calm my nerves. Usually I go home with Alex, but he didn't wait for me. Nothing's happening. I'd really like something to happen.

Instead of going straight home, I take the rue Ramponeau instead, and end up on the rue de Belleville. I look around me in every direction. There are Chinese restaurants with grilled chickens hanging in the window. There are appetisers I don't know. So I'm just walking around, noticing all this. One day, I'd really like to go to a restaurant. But M'am says that it's like throwing money out of the window of a train.

Then something did happen. I saw Lolita. She's with Johanne. They're walking on the other side of the street. I cross the street so they'll recognise me. But maybe they're busy, and they don't see me. I follow them. They're chattering. Lolita is swinging her bag just like a lady. It comes and goes, comes and goes, it touches her dress and makes a kind of wave in her dress. In any case, she is wonderful.

Lolita enters No 65, which leads into an inside courtyard. Lolita's house is the one with a bay window and white curtains on the second floor. I saw her hanging over the balcony once, that's how I know. But Lolita didn't see me. I'd love to live in a house like this. I took out a piece of paper and made a drawing. I wanted to slide it under Lolita's door. Who cares, I finally said to myself. She wouldn't even know it's me.

I had the drawing in my hand and was looking at Lolita's window. While I was waiting, two cops on the beat came by. I got scared but didn't budge, seeing that if you begin to run you're guilty without trial. So I watched Lolita's window, no expression on my face. The cop saw my drawing.

'What's that, a toad?'

'No, it's a dog.'

He looks at me. He takes my drawing, shows it to his partner. They burst out laughing.

'You nuts or what?' he asks me.

'Yes, sir.'

'You can expect anything with these niggers.'

'Sir, give me back my drawing.'

'Ah! that's a laugh,' he goes.

But I'm not in a laughing mood. I jump up and grab my drawing.

'Calm down, you little shit!'

'Stop bugging him,' the other cop says.

I raise my head and see Lolita. She saw me and called out:

'Oh what a gutsy boy!'

◆

At home the women are talking. They get up, they're chattering. They wash the floor, they're chattering, they cook, they're chattering.

'He's there and I can't believe my eyes,' goes Soumana.

'I told you so. You've just gotta wait.'

'But it doesn't change the fact that I want to leave.'

'And go where? You don't know anyone.'

'I'll manage. I'm no worse than those who show their arse in the films.'

M'am smiles. And then Soumana pushes her toothpick into the side of her cheek and gets angry.

She leaves, and when she comes back into the kitchen, she looks like I've never seen her look before. She's wearing a hat that doesn't suit her 'cause it couldn't anyway. She's put on a pair of trousers, grey with a Prince of Wales check, that gives her an arse beyond description since it takes up every bit of space. She's holding her crocodile bag. She still has it from Africa and keeps it for sentimental reasons, which I know about very well. She's looking at us with an air of elegance, like a stranger, someone who has never had to wait on anyone.

M'am looks her up and down and then says to her:

'You'd better take that off before he gets here.'

'Never! Abdou likes me a lot in trousers. When we first met I had

60

red ones. That really turned him on. Like a bull, if you see what I mean.'

And then she smiles. You'd think someone had just brought her some good news. Her eyes drift off to some faraway place. You can see she's thinking rose-coloured thoughts, and on and on. Thoughts like paradise. M'am raises her shoulders and lets them drop again.

'I do believe I can become a film actress,' Soumana says, as she puts one hand on her hip and flutters her lashes.

'And why not the queen of England?'

'I hadn't thought of that. But they do go together.'

She is silent. She throws her head back and continues:

'After all, that's how Grace Kelly met Prince Rainier.'

'That's right,' M'am says, doubled up with laughter. 'Don't forget to send me an invitation.'

'And how're you going to become an actress?' I ask.

'I'll go to Cannes. The producers are down there. One of them will fall in love, and then . . .'

She went on talking as if to herself.

'In Cannes, there's the sea, there are English lords who take walks along the beach, there are boats, birds, clowns in the street, balloons falling from the sky, and princesses of Monaco who romp around on the beach in their swimsuits. I'll have gorgeous dresses, fur coats, cars, jewellery . . .'

'And get plenty of abuse,' M'am goes, laughing.

'Never will I let him lay a finger on me. You heard what Madame Saddock said! Let him just try to raise his hand to me and I'll shove every woman in France up his arse.'

She hadn't finished what she was saying, when father comes home. He's not alone. My uncle Kouam is with him.

When they see Soumana dressed like that, my uncle covers his mouth with his hand so as not to laugh. Dad looks at her as if she were a pile of dirt. With eyes that say: 'What is this monstrosity?'

'Take that off!' my dad says.

'*I no be talk!*' M'am says.

Soumana lowers her head. She left to get changed. But before she disappeared, I saw her eyes. It wasn't pleasant. All of Africa's demons were there.

61

They sat down and M'am served them mint tea. My dad broke a cola nut. He gave a sliver to my uncle Kouam.

'I wonder what I should do to get Mathilda to listen to me,' he explains to my father. 'She does only what comes into her head. She never obeys and, what's more, she talks back. In the evening, if she wants to go out with friends, she just goes. I tell her we're married and that, well, after all, her place is by my side. She answers that it makes no difference. "If you want to come along, all you have to do is come. Leave me alone!" She gets all tarted up in front of the mirror, she's whistling. I don't know what to do any more . . .'

'All you have to do is to give her one! That's the only thing that works with women. You beat her. You f . . . her. Then you can die in peace.'

My uncle Kouam is looking at his hands. He's embarrassed.

'I can't,' he says in a little voice.

'So, don't complain then . . .'

'I just think there's got to be another way.'

'So find it without me.'

Then there was a long, heavy silence. My dad spat, *splat*!

Sitting on a chair in the kitchen, Soumana is crying. All her clothes have fallen down. Not really, of course. But it's a way of saying that she's really had it. She's completely deflated. M'am is making dinner, yams with brisket. She doesn't look at her. Nobody could teach her again how to live, even if you liked her a lot. That is to say, to walk without thinking about walking, to eat without thinking about eating, and to laugh like a baby entranced by the jingling of a bracelet. Nobody can give her back her youth. I take her hand. That's all I can do for her.

◆

Afterwards, I went out into the street, I felt like taking a walk. I crossed paths with Monsieur Ndongala.

'So, my little Loukoum, how's it going?'

'Very well, Monsieur Ndongala,' I answer. 'And what about you?'

'As long as you're a nigger in this place, there's nothing you can do about it!'

Monsieur Ndongala is very nice and handsome like no one else. Only the French police don't look too kindly upon him because he attracts crowds. He says he's waiting for the right moment and then he'll go back to Africa to cram a lot of information into the skulls of the people down there. He says that the Africans are just like the white people. They all believe they're the centre of the universe. When chiefs make roads, they think it's for their own benefit, though they don't even have a car. When you look at him carefully, Monsieur Ndongala is made to be a king, to have people bow and scrape to him, and to kick them in the arse. He'd do well in Bokassa's place. I always bite my tongue so as not to say this, seeing as no one asks for my opinion.

I actually quite like Monsieur Ndongala, because he won't be messed with. When he gathers a crowd and the police come, he doesn't stop talking, and if someone asks him something, he says: 'My papers are in order'. And then he goes on talking and nobody can do a thing to him since his student papers are beyond reproach.

'How's your wife?' I ask.

He looks at me as if he were dreaming.

'Which one?'

I think this over and then say:

'The one with the frosted hair.'

'Sonya?'

'Yeah.'

'Gone.'

'And why'd she leave?'

'When a woman gets married, she's there to keep house and take care of her children. You should've seen it! Filthy house. The kid unwashed. Runny nose. Disgusting. I didn't even dare touch her any more.'

'You could do it, the work . . .'

'Noooo! That's woman's work . . . What's more, she didn't know how to cook.'

'I rather liked her lemon tart,' I say. 'After all, maybe it's good she didn't want to stay . . .'

He is very philosophical, at least he laughed. Then he says:

'Why don't you come by the house one of these days. I'll introduce you to Patricia, my new woman. She makes a chocolate cream like nobody else!'

'Yeah, one of these days,' I answer, my hands in my pockets.

One of these days . . .

Why a woman, you'll say to me? Why women? The love of women guides me through my memories. They are my legends. I have married that legend. And in my madness, woman is like a lantern. A small exiled moon. She is my only wisdom.

You know, friend, exclusion is built into the system. No, you can't know this, too involved with your own kind. I see you smiling at life. You speak of tenderness, being made giddy by the one perfume. One and only one woman. Even her betrayals gratify you. But these easy paths are not open to me. So, listen:

Hatred.

Violence.

Or indifference.

Work that robs life of every moment.

Crimes.

Raids.

Searches.

They don't kill. They humiliate. They destroy.

So I curl up in those magical sheets in which woman weaves me thousands and thousands of dreams, on the other side of the wounds. She teaches me the legends anew and I ejaculate my tenderness in the wind.

Woman is my drug. I never get tired of it.

Fragile hours resounding with hope,

From which I hollow out my frenzy so I can coil up inside it.

This body of woman is my heaven, my wealth, my permanent miracle. It's not a theft, friend, anyway your wife doesn't look at me. Take it easy, I'm on the negotiable path. I've been given the grace to escape from the burden, to consider that weight as a frame for a mirror.

65

My words are crazy. You think so.

Your legend tells you that I'm incapable of loving, that my horse-sized genitals creep into my brain, suffocate my intelligence, and implant stupidity there. I won't take ten thousand years of prejudices out of your skull. Life's anguish separates me from you. But if you were to place your bed for one single night on the pathways of insomnia, transforming the sleep that's escaping you into one long dark day, well then my life will reach you.

(Abdou Traoré)

Mademoiselle Garnier took us for the natural science lesson. First she talked. She said that animals are grouped into two families: the vertebrates and the invertebrates, cold-blooded and warm-blooded; there are useful and harmful animals. Mammals are the most evolved on the scale of living creatures, primates the most evolved of the mammals, and humans are at the top and dominate everything because they have language. That doesn't thrill me as a theory. I really wonder where my family gets categorised.

We went to the zoo. Mademoiselle Garnier lined us up. We moved forward two by two in a neat little line. We were holding hands. The sheep of Panurge, as Monsieur Ndongala would say. Mademoiselle Garnier doesn't stop yelling: 'Hold hands! Stay close to me!' She's terrified of losing a child and I think to myself she's going to end up by losing her head.

It's crowded in the underground. Nobody is talking except for the schoolchildren who are shouting. There's an aroma in the métro that hangs on like a stale cushion of air. The longer we travel, the more intense it becomes. As for me, I fan myself with my notebook. Behind us the tracks disappear and I along with them. I don't know why but it's a weird feeling. Suddenly an old woman appears in front of Sylvain Durand and me. She really looks like a madwoman, with her striped trousers and her navy blue mechanic's jacket. She has three hairs on her head so you can read her thoughts right through her skull, that's why I personally think she's crazy.

'It's fantastic!' she says. 'I'm on holiday.'

66

Then she sits down directly across from us.

'I'm the boss of a company,' she says. 'It's fantastic to take time off while you make the workers sweat for you. What do the masses want?' she asks.

The kids snigger. Mademoiselle Garnier immediately begins to yell: 'Calm down, Madame! Calm down, Madame.'

'Wouldn't think of it!' says the old lady. 'I bought a house for 150,000 francs with a friend. Of course, I didn't buy it all by myself! We have to pay it off at 1500 francs a month; weird, don't you think?'

'I agree with you,' I answer her.

'Be quiet, Loukoum,' says Mademoiselle Garnier.

'He's free to talk,' yells the old lady. 'You should let children speak.'

'Thank you, Madame,' I say to her, ''cause where I come from, children don't have the right to talk.'

'Well now! How about that! I, for one, say that's not normal, not at all! Not at all! Come with me, come with me,' she says.

Then she starts pulling me by the arm.

'Come, little boy, come on little boy. I'll protect you.'

'I'll call the police,' Mademoiselle Garnier threatens.

'You can call God himself if you want,' says the old madwoman. 'In this country, there's no way those rights can be denied, so if you call the good Lord, that might be better. He'd find some solutions.'

She's talking so loud and hard that her spittle lands right in my face. And me, I look like a wet rooster with drops of spit on my face. Everybody is sniggering. 'Loukoum sti-inks! Loukoum sti-inks!' Even Lolita. From where I was I couldn't see her, but my heart heard the laughter in her throat. Then she stretched her neck and showed me her face, and I felt something like tenderness all the way down in the bottom of my heart; it moved, moved, then moved some more. A woman is really something else, even if it brings confusion.

◆

In the zoo, there are trees and fences so that Paris won't turn into a virgin forest like down there in Africa, where animals have complete freedom to eat people. It truly is absolutely typical of white people to have houses for each animal, except they have no roof above their huts and there is only the sky. If it weren't cold some of the time, I'd love to have a house without a roof so I could talk directly to the stars. There are paths with arrows and signs marked 'Monkeys' or 'African lions' and so on. We visited them. There were also chimpanzees, who were looking for lice in each other's hair. They stick them in their mouths and eat them; I watched and watched, because I thought that only women looked for lice on the heads of other people, like down there in Africa, where my dad was so full of lice that my grandmother, whom I don't know, would say to him all the time: 'Come here so I can kill your lice!'

Then we went to see the camels, the turtles, the gazelles, and the porcupines. But I saw nothing at all, seeing as they were sleeping inside a hole. Then Mademoiselle Garnier said:

'Time to eat, children.'

All the kids sat down in the rest area. They took out their lunch bags. There were filled chocolate bars which I don't like. Raisin cakes and vanilla cake, and many other things which I love, but which M'am didn't give me, worried she wouldn't be considered thrifty. I took out my corn cake. It was full of palm oil and dripping everywhere between my fingers. That's when Lolita planted herself in front of me:

'What's that you're eating?' she asks, with curiosity not disgust.

'Corn cakes,' I tell her.

'Can I taste?' she asks.

Suddenly I can't move. It's as if I'm nailed to the spot, right there. I look into her eyes and my heart says: 'Anything you want, princess, anything you want.'

'You don't have to give her anything if you don't want to,' Alex says.

He doesn't even have time to finish his sentence when I say, almost too quickly:

'But I want to give her my cakes.'

Mademoiselle Garnier looks at me as if I were cooking up something evil inside my head. The kids are whispering stuff, then they burst out laughing.

Lolita eats the cake and says: 'It's wonderful!' Then she wipes her fingers on her dress.

Very soon Mademoiselle Garnier said:

'Clean up, children. It's time to visit more animals.'

We went off to see other animals. There were all kinds. Panthers with teeth like wolves. It's not true that panthers have teeth like wolves, but my dad always says: 'That one, don't trust him, he's a wolf!'

Alex began to walk on all fours beside me.

'What's your problem?'

'My mother recognised me,' he tells me.

'Oh yeah? You ran into her?'

'Yeah,' he goes. 'There she is.'

'Where?'

He didn't say anything. He showed me a zebra and her calf. And me, I felt embarrassed, as embarrassed as you always feel when you've been taken in. But that's Alex's speciality. One day, when we were very small, we still had all our baby teeth, he stole Marabout Cérif's blessed liquid; this is what comes off the hardwood tablet when the secret writing is washed off. Alex quietly poured the hardwood water into Monsieur Guillaume's whisky bottle. In the end, all the customers were saying: 'Oh, hardwood gives you a hard-on!' He really knows the art of getting you all worked into a stew.

We went to see the elephants. They place their trunks majestically on the ground to snap up their food which they then put in their mouth. Their big ears hang slack like great balls. I don't know why, but I've always thought that elephants are the true kings of the forest. There's nothing like them anywhere, except perhaps in Africa. Monsieur Ndongala says the Africans are so stupid they're killing all the elephants to sell their trunks to the white people. It seems that they even sell off whole villages. So then the whites give them orders. They say: 'Cut your trees!' and the Africans obey. They cut down the giant baobabs, the mahogany trees, in short, just about everything! Seems that soon there won't even be any shade down there in which to rest and live life to the full.

I also thought of Soumana. It's true though! As an elephant she would have lived her life without worrying about all that being overweight. But she isn't an elephant. We all should have been able to choose whatever we wanted to be. Me, I would have liked being a bird. An eagle. I never would have felt any horror. I would fly over everything philosophically.

Then I took a walk down the lane into dimly lit spots. At the bend of the path, I see Lolita. From the back. Maybe she's not busy? I don't budge. I wait. Useless trying to induce happiness. It is strong enough to move of its own accord and pay me a visit.

'Don't you like elephants?' Lolita asks me.

'Sure I do,' I tell her.

'You're lying,' she says to me.

'No, I'm not!'

'You're like all the other guys,' she says. 'You lie all the time. When your friends are there, you put on airs.'

'No, I don't!'

'Yes, you do. I just saw you there with Alex. You even pretend girls don't interest you, but you don't stop looking at me and at all the others, too.'

Inch Allah!

At last it was time to leave.

When we came back to the classroom, Mademoiselle Garnier said:

'You're on holiday from now until the sixth of January.'

'Yippee!' we all yelled.

'Steady, children,' went Mademoiselle Garnier.

'Just one moment!. . . School isn't over yet.'

'Ooooh!'

Then she giggled and said:

'Enjoy your holiday, children. And a Merry Christmas!'

We all filed out. I was the last one to leave the class.

◆

In the schoolyard, I saw Lolita. There she is in the sun waiting for me. She's waiting for me and I feel all warm in my belly. And me, I slow down my steps on purpose to let her wait for me. When I reach her, Pierre Pelletier is also approaching and she holds out her little hands, small as stars, to him. I gather it's not me she's waiting for, but Pierre Pelletier; that's only normal, he's smarter than me so . . .!

◆

First I hung around for a bit. I looked at the pigeons in the Belleville gardens. In the Belleville gardens, there are black women with their crowds of kids. They're wearing *pagnes* blooming with birds, elephants, zebras. They are a garden.

First I hung around for a bit. I looked at the pigeons in the Belleville gardens. In the Belleville gardens, there are black women with their crowds of kids. They're wearing *pagnes* blooming with birds, elephants, zebras. They are a garden.

Suddenly I see Madame Saddock. She's with a gentleman. She doesn't look happy. She's talking loud and waving her arms around. You'd think any moment she's going to throw a pie in his face. The gentleman says nothing. He's walking slowly, his hands folded behind his back. Every now and then he shakes his head as if to say: sure . . . OK . . . yes, I understand . . .

Shit! I think that woman isn't very nice. To talk that way to a guy, with a cigarette in her mouth and it doesn't even embarrass her!

Inch Allah! You won't see such a sight among blacks!

I skip off to Monsieur Guillaume's café. The whole black clan is there. A few Arabs are sitting around. They're sneaking looks at every chick that comes by. They make comments, they snigger. Personally, I don't see anything funny in it.

I'm thinking of Lolita. I'm wondering why she chased after me only to drop me like a hot potato. It must be said, women sometimes are a treacherous lot. I'm certainly not going to contradict that myth. It's really crappy, though!

I don't even feel like a Coke. Monsieur Guillaume offers a Fanta. Not the same thing. I refuse. I close my eyes. I open them. I was still there. When you're alive that's how it has to be.

I hear a:

'Ooooh! Isn't that impressive?'

It's Monsieur Laforêt. He makes a very showy entrance, dressed like a king. His jacket is black. His trousers are grey, held up by braces. A bow tie. And a fancy label coat. It creates an uproar because nobody has ever seen him clean, closely shaven; and smelling of cologne from three metres away.

He put his hands in his pockets. He went to the bar, strutting a little, and he said:

'This round's on me.'

Nobody reacted positively. Everyone is hysterical. I run over to the bar and say: 'Monsieur Laforêt!' as I hold out my hand. But in no time there's a big black woman in red shorts, showing all her teeth, who jumps on him. And before I can ask who this fat teddybear is, she says:

'Monsieur Laforêt, I *am* glad to see you! Monsieur Kaba has told me *so* much about you that I feel as if I've known you for ever.'

Monsieur Kaba, with a smile, hangs back a little.

'This is Rosette,' he goes. 'The new one.'

'Hi everyone,' she says.

Then she puts one hand around Monsieur Laforêt's neck. She looks at him, raising her head, as if she finds him very handsome, and then she stands on tiptoe and kisses him.

I watch Monsieur Guillaume out of the corner of my eye. He looks as if the sky has come down on his head. I'm not much better.

'This is my Christmas present to you, that I've brought to congratulate you,' goes Monsieur Kaba.

He's smoking his fat cigar. He blows the smoke towards the ceiling. He watches the line that the smoke sketches in the air. He laughs suddenly, then goes on:

'When a man works all the time, he needs something to buck him up. Especially in the winter.'

Monsieur Kaba approaches Monsieur Laforêt, the cigar in his smiling mouth. He takes his hand with an affectionate gesture.

'We've got a lot to talk about, eh, old boy?' He turns to Rosette: 'Leave us alone for a moment, my dear. Go on, go away . . . And be good!'

'Yeah, sure!' she goes, looking annoyed.

Then he turns back to Monsieur Laforêt.

'Here we are, both businessmen now, yes, businessmen. Well, what do you say?'

Nobody seems to notice that I'm there. I sit down. I'm in a really good spot. I can't ask for anything more. At that very moment, a group of white men came in and yelled:

'Nobody move! Police!'

Somebody said: 'Shit!'

'Everybody, face the wall!'

Monsieur Kaba throws his glass on the floor and at the same time shoves his hands in his pockets. Fortunately, I had time to hide under a table, or else it would have landed on me. In the time it takes me to stick my neck back out to see what's going on, he's already three steps away from the door.

'Don't move, I said,' the inspector goes. 'Turn around quietly, face the wall!'

'Never in my life!' screams Monsieur Ndongala. 'I am an honest citizen, I am!'

'What did you say to Inspector Harry?' a cop asks as he points his pistol at his nose.

'First, I want to know the charges.'

'With pleasure . . .' says the inspector. 'Frisk 'em all.'

'Boss, we've got our man,' yells a cop as he grabs Monsieur Laforêt by the collar.

'Strange characters you've got in this dump of yours,' the inspector goes, as he looks at Monsieur Guillaume.

'What do you want, Inspector, it's not my job to ask questions! With cops like you, every Frenchman can sleep soundly.'

After that I can't go on and tell you any more. My eyes are filled with tears and I've got a lump in my throat. Poor Monsieur Kaba tries to make himself look small and is trembling like a leaf.

Mademoiselle Rosette jumps up and runs to find refuge at the bar. A cop yanks her by the arm.

'Hey, easy . . .'

She smacks him one. The cop throws her on the ground and beats her up.

He straightens up and says:

'That's a real dangerous lunatic, that one.'

'Yes, Inspector,' my uncle Kaba answers. 'I've been telling her for years to be careful of her nerves. You know what women are like . . .'

'Yeah. You're going to tell us all about it at the station. Put them in the car.'

They took everybody away, hands on their heads. Only Monsieur Ndongala put his fists in the air and shouted:

'I'll take this to my lawyer!'

73

'Yeah, right. Move it!'

Suddenly he notices I'm there.

'Hey, you brat, what the hell are you up to here, you? Get out!'

I go out and then watch them until they've been taken away.

◆

'People are crazy, all of them,' says my dad. 'How do you want things to work out on this earth if you can't even have a drink without being thrown in the clink?'

We're all sitting around the table. My dad is chewing his cola nut and spits *splat!* on the floor.

'We've got to get them out of there,' says my dad.

'Any ideas?' my uncle Kouam asks.

Monsieur Guillaume is scratching his chin. You have to understand: he has no more customers to keep him busy.

'We should threaten them, tell 'em we're leaving France,' my dad suggests.

'They'll really be sorry to see you go, old man!' M'am sniggers.

'Maybe they will,' my dad says. 'What if we went on strike? The French won't stand for it, not having any street-cleaners. They'll be forced to satisfy our request.'

'Don't even think about it,' says Monsieur Guillaume. 'They don't give a fuck about niggers, so . . . They'll only use it to throw you out even faster without any compensation. Don't forget, the Rumanians are watching and waiting. They'll be quite happy to replace you.'

Then everybody falls silent. I really wonder what they're thinking about. Me, I'm thinking about Blanco, my winged horse, the one I invented in my head. I climb on top of him as in the passage in the Bible which Monsieur Guillaume never stops telling us about. This is what he says, that one day there will be so much sin on earth that an angel will come on his white horse and that it will have wings like the birds do. He'll be so furious that he'll crush everything in his way, even the buildings. And as for me, I'm on Blanco, I am that angel, except it isn't entirely me, I'll rip out the private houses and let all the homeless of Belleville stay there, all those who don't know who they are any more because nobody looks at them at all. And everybody will look at them now and *they* will give the orders. When I think about it, though, I wonder if that's any better, because in the end the others will be rich instead and will do nothing but stupid stuff in turn.

'What's his name, the head commissioner?' asks my dad.

'Dellacqua,' answers my uncle Kouam.

'I want his mother's name.'

'What for?'

'I want to get rid of her,' my dad says.

That's when my aunt Mathilda says:

'Your black magic won't work.'

'Oh really?' goes my dad. 'And what do you suggest?'

'Somebody should go and negotiate with him.'

'Hmmm!' goes my dad. 'But who?'

He settles back in his armchair. He breaks a nut. He chews it. He spits, *splat splat*.

'I have the solution,' he says.

Everyone looks at him.

'Yeah. I figured out who should negotiate with him.'

He closes his eyes, opens them suddenly and points at my aunt Mathilda, crying:

'You should!'

'Me? Why me?'

'Your papers are in order, you're a woman, you're white, so everything is in your favour.'

'Not my wife!' yells uncle Kouam. 'You're not really going to send my wife into the lion's den, are you!'

'What about solidarity? What'll you do about that, my brother?'

'I . . .' stammers my uncle Kouam.

It was all set. M'am knew it, that's why she said:

'I'm going to pray so that the good Lord will speak through your mouth.'

Inch Allah.

◆

The next morning, my aunt Mathilda got dressed up and went off to see the commissioner. She hadn't been gone ten minutes when we see

75

the entire black tribe come tearing out. With haggard eyes, stinking breath, their hair a mess, but they're holding out.

'Really,' my dad goes, ' she sure works fast, that wife of yours . . .'

'Yeah,' answers my uncle, not looking too happy.

'We're free!' they all shout, laughing.

Monsieur Kaba approaches and asks my dad:

'You wouldn't by any chance have a piece of cola? Those pricks took all my cigars.'

My dad gives him a piece of cola.

'So?'

'So what?' asks Monsieur Kaba.

'What happened?'

'Bah, they asked a lot of questions. I know them by heart by now, you know. They put us in the slammer. And this morning, they set us free.'

'I don't see Monsieur Laforêt,' my dad goes.

'They're holding him.'

'Tell me.'

'Well, they found some papers on him that belong to a guy who lodged a complaint against him for theft. So they kept him.'

'Shit!'

'Don't fret. It's between whites. He can get off with three months locked up.'

Then everyone laughed. They shook each other's hands. They danced, then drank to everybody's health. I've never seen such a bunch of madmen.

Two hours later, my aunt Mathilda comes back. She's seen better days. Her lips are white and yet she'd put on plenty of lipstick before leaving. After all, if she talked that much with the commissioner . . .

'Hey, my darling,' my uncle cries, 'look who's here?'

When she sees the black tribe, her eyes nearly pop out of her head. She opens her mouth, too, but closes it again immediately.

'Congratulations, my dear,' says dad, smacking a kiss on her cheek. 'Good work.'

'Yeah,' goes Monsieur Guillaume. 'You're a genius, little one. You really owe her a great deal, guys . . .'

'Thanks! thanks!' the niggers yell.

But she doesn't seem to hear. She pulls up a chair and sits down next to me.

'Have they been here long?' she asks me.

'Yes, aunt,' I say.

She sighs deeply and mutters something.

'What d'you say?' asks my dad.

She lowers her head and puts her face between her hands. Then she shouts:

'The bastard!'

I walk the streets. I dream up the past.

The tree in the courtyard, my neighbour's cat, the bougainvillaea climbing up the wall, the women, the children running through the compounds and the hammock stretched between two mango trees. Memories of a time that has been erased by social impotence, memories I have lived.

You, friend, you pass by and do not see me. It is true that I do not exist. I am a transparency, a sheet of paper borne away by the wind. A car almost carried me off. The driver growled. He raised a threatening arm. He wants to destroy me, a leaf that's getting away from him. I dissolved his rage in a bath of laughter.

I would very much like to tell you about my country in a way that is different from what you've read in books. I know that you won't believe me. And yet I am suffering and I no longer know where to place my anguish.

I run to seek refuge in this metallic coffin, MY HOUSE.

The women spy on my every step. They open the door without my even having to knock. I'm never surprised at that door opening as if by magic. I am used to it and I know that these guardians of love are always standing in wait. Yes, and to such a point that their eyes, which scrutinise my health and my worries, sometimes antagonise me. Sometimes I resent their looking after me too much.

They. Women. They know how to invent me, they also know how to adopt me, to reinvent me. I, who am only a breath, madness anchored inside the skulls of idiots ... And in a flight of mumbled words, the women recreate me. Their fingers, spread wide, settle into my hair. I travel over their bodies which open up to my tenderness and I fall asleep, inside the open arms of heaven. Exile moves away.

(Abdou Traoré)

Madame Saddock, as you can tell by just looking at her, is a ballbreaker of the first order, someone who smells nasty though she may be the most perfumed woman in the whole of Belleville. But it's true! What does she want to be prophesying that grand women's revolution for? It has done a lot of good here in France, but it is a natural disaster among the immigrants. Say what you like but in France women have suffered sexual racism. They have their reasons! But Soumana and M'am have never had to complain of being badly treated sexually. There's never been a tragedy or a corpse. So I don't quite see what Madame Saddock is waiting for. Well, as my dad says, with women you never know . . .

And that's just it, Madame Saddock won't leave us alone! She comes to see the women twice a week and brings them presents: perfume, sweets, cakes, lipstick . . . But what suits Soumana best are the perfumes, because that allows her to forget her excess kilos. You should try to understand if you can. But not everything works that way. Better begin at the beginning.

First of all, Madame Saddock makes sure my dad isn't there, seeing how he'd throw her out on her ear if he caught her being a bad influence. So she stands on the pavement over the road. She puts two fingers in her mouth and whistles. Soumana opens the window and signals for her to come upstairs. Then Madame Saddock comes in and sits down in my dad's armchair or she stands against the door with her hands folded. She explains to the women what rights they have, and the whole great tale-for-women-who-don't-get-laid-enough. When she talks, she gestures, gets upset, and even ends up by becoming seriously angry. Not because she's furious, but because she wants to say even more, and my mothers with their limited means up top can't always understand what she's talking about. She'd need diamond words to cram their skulls full of all the marvellous things of life, or so she thinks. If you want my opinion, that woman has no feeling. Which doesn't help her mood at all. And that Soumana listens to her religiously and confides in her, even though some of it is too shameful to be told. She tells Madame Saddock my dad is a good-for-nothing, a skirt-chaser, a grave-digger, that he has horribly compromised his fancy dreams, and that she's had enough of it! That she's really sick of being treated this way. Listening to her, you'd think she is a champion victim of ill treatment and deserves the Nobel Prize for the most rejected woman in the world. M'am doesn't say a whole lot. She stays crouched on her mat like a giant baobab tree, chewing on her toothpick. And Madame Saddock frets. She yells:

'In your place I'd go here, I'd do this, I'd do that.'

That's just it, though, she isn't in their place, she has no business sticking her nose in what's theirs. African marriages – she doesn't have a clue what they're all about. She doesn't understand the first thing about the way we live. And the other day I got mad and told her:

'I'll tell my dad everything.'

'What'll you tell your dad?' Madame Saddock asked laughingly, but I wasn't in the mood for jokes and answered:

'I'll tell my father that Soumana uses bad words when he isn't here.'

'It's not nice to repeat what you hear, Loukoum.'

'I'm telling him anyway,' I went sulkily.

'Why would you do a thing like that?'

''Cause it isn't nice to say nasty things.'

'So?'

'It doesn't cost a thing to be nice,' I told her.

'But he isn't nice either, your dad.'

'Yes he is.'

'He is mean to Sou.'

'That's not true! And I'll tell him so.'

'You'll say nothing of the sort!' Sou scolded. 'If you say one single word then I'll tell him that you read his magazines.'

'Sometimes I look at the pictures. I like looking at the clothes. They're elegant.'

'What magazines are you talking about?' Madame Saddock asked.

'Photographs. Of naked women!' answered Soumana.

'That pig!' says Madame Saddock. 'What a heap of shit!'

'You shouldn't say "shit",' I told her. 'It's a dirty word.'

But she got up and said:

'Shit! Shit! Shit!'

Then she went to the door, turned around, looked at me and said again:

'I'll say dirty words whenever I feel like it, Loukoum. We live in a free country.'

I was in a stinking bad mood. I didn't know what to do. So I pretended I was a cowboy, pointed at her with the finger you shouldn't point with, went *bang-bang!* and killed her.

Nobody reacted for several minutes. Then Madame Saddock said:

'Now there's one I wouldn't want my daughter to marry.'

M'am looked at her, looked at her, looked at her again, then said:

'Sometimes we think we understand, but it's not as simple as that. And, really, Allah isn't crazy!'

That woman really is a saint!

Inch Allah!

◆

In the end I said nothing to my dad about Madame Saddock and her bad influence. He didn't ask me anything, so ... But I'm quite sure that I'm in for it and that one of these days it will come down on us without any warning.

I go shopping with M'am in the department stores near the Opéra. There's a circus in the shop windows. Parents come to look at it with their kids and it's free. The window is framed in stars that are bigger than in real life. They light up and go off in the twinkling of an eye. In the middle of the circus there are astronauts. They go all the way to heaven, come back to earth while they greet the passers-by. There's a Santa Claus on the poster with toys. He looks like the good Lord. He is white with a great big beard. I look at Santa Claus, it's as if I'm in heaven. With all those white, white angels, their white hair, their white eyes, you'd think they were albinos. The angels are beating their huge cymbals and one of them is blowing into its trumpet. God opens his hand. Lots and lots of toys come falling down.

I watch, and watch, and watch. I don't want to go away. But M'am pulls me by my jacket and says:

'Hurry up, your father will be getting home soon.'

We leave again. There are lots of people everywhere, dressed as if for work. They're running. They're bumping into each other. They're pushing each other. They excuse themselves. Sometimes a lady's packages slip and scatter all over the ground. She bends down to pick them up. I see between her legs.

At one point, when I raise my eyes, I look up to discover a whole crowd gathered there. I'm curious to know what's going on. I really wonder if … And M'am goes toward the spot where the people are congregating like flies. I want to have a taste of it, too. Snatch their thoughts.

There's a black man standing on a platform. He is African. I'm fairly sure he is from Sarcelles. I don't know where that is, but my friend Ahmidou, whom you don't know, told me that in Saint-Denis they bring all the black people together to register their names and then, one day, they'll throw them on charter planes and send them back to Mali.

The black man is holding a white flag in his hands. Dozens of people are listening to him. The black man is saying that black people don't know they're black. You all want to be white, but the whites can see very clearly from your looks that you're not from this soil. Caribbean? That doesn't mean a thing! We're all African … Africa, that's our roots. Nobody can deny his origins without heading for disaster. The orator is shouting. You'd think someone was trying to pick a fight with him. He shouts:

'Wake up! Defend yourselves! The Monster has come! He's going to kill your children! He's going to rape your women! He has a face: the face of the National Front! Wake up all of you and be black together! No more Africans! No more Americans! No more Caribbeans! Everybody black! Learn a new song! Sing the anthem of solidarity!'

The black man shouts. He must be of the same age as Monsieur Ndongala. He is well dressed. Do black people really believe they're not black? He seems to be looking at me. He is looking at me. He points his finger at me and says:

'Women, do not listen to those who proclaim family planning. Have children! Reproduce yourselves! For when the great day comes, your children will be your salvation! Thousands of black people will come forth from …'

I didn't hear the end. M'am said:

'Come on, we've got to go. The packages are getting heavy.'

We took the métro. When we arrived home, M'am threw the parcels down and sat on her mat and told Soumana what the black man had been saying. Soumana began to cry.

And she cries. Her face is tense. You'd think it's going to tear apart like an old rag.

I don't know what to do. M'am takes her hand and I watch her cry. Then she gets tired. She no longer cries. But she's not moving either. She's cold. M'am holds her close and she begins to talk!

'My mum didn't like men, I didn't understand why. She couldn't even stand the least little physical touch.'

'Yet, she did have kids,' Soumana says.

'Twelve. I imagine my dad had to force her, unless she accepted that she had nothing better to do. As soon as a man came anywhere near me, she'd say: "Go to the kitchen right now, Maryam".'

Maryam is M'am's real name. But everyone calls her M'am and I think it suits her well.

'As for my dad, he, well he was a strutting cock, worse than Abdou, can you imagine? I'm sure he could have slept with a sow if it had been appetising. Next to him, Abdou is a joke.'

'You're very lenient,' Soumana says.

'Not at all! Why get yourself in such a state as soon as . . .'

'Stop!' Soumana says. 'I don't want to hear any of it.'

'Exactly! When I first knew Abdou, he needed six women a day. Different ones. And he'd do it anywhere. In the chicken coop, in the corn or millet fields, in a tree. You realise that? A real true cock. He's calmed down a bit.'

'Dear God, what do I have to listen to?'

'I swear to you, Sou! But he loved me. Really. We had tremendous fun together. He taught me everything.'

'Fat lot of good that does you!'

'When I became pregnant, and right away too, my parents threw me out. I went to live with an aunt, my mother's sister. She was fun, she was. The men, she ruled them with an iron rod because she ran a place to eat and had a bit of money, and in Africa, men today like women who have money better than the others. My mum had contempt for her. She always used to say that my aunt would spread her legs any time, no matter how, no matter for whom. But why isn't it acceptable that women, too, have themselves a good time?'

M'am bursts out laughing.

'And why didn't I manage to cheat on Abdou with everything he did

83

to me? Perhaps because I love him. Maybe that's it, maybe. Unless it's my parents who filled my skull with crap I can't manage to forget. It's like gangrene! It eats away at you and then you find yourself dead without even being aware of it. Maybe if I'd been able to make some babies after that, Abdou wouldn't have left me. Actually, what do I know? Nothing. And then again, he's changed a lot. Physically he's not the same man. He doesn't laugh as much as before. He does things that make you wonder if he's still all there. I think it's because we're so far away from Mali. Because before, despite everything, we really were very good together. When you came, it hurt me a lot, but when the kids were born it wasn't the same any more! Sometimes I wonder what could have happened to him. How come he no longer takes me for a walk? How come we no longer look at the sunset together? That he doesn't even try to do it with me any more?'

But Sou was no longer talking. It was as if she'd died inside. Then M'am stopped speaking. She touched Sou's forehead. She said:

'I think you've got a fever.'

M'am gave her a pill and put her to bed.

Then she went into the kitchen to prepare dinner.

◆

At that moment something terrible happened. Really. Someone rang the doorbell. And I went to open it.

There stood a very pretty and even attractive woman, except for her eyes which looked like the eyes of a dog that's just been kicked in the arse. I don't know her, never seen her before, not even as a special protégée of Monsieur Kaba's. She's not dark. I mean that she's pale and breathing quickly, with one hand on her heart seeing that staircases are not kind to a heart unused to them. She's wearing a coat made of some kind of skin, like fur. But it isn't real fur. She's really dolled up. A very short, black leather skirt with a little jacket that leaves her belly bare, like a tart. That's what M'am calls it, a tart, a girl worth nothing at all. She looks at me closely as if she's checking something inside my nose and I give it right back to her, for it's enough just to see that woman, with her tits, for God's sake! to understand that things are going to blow up and you'll pay for it in every way.

'Monsieur Abdou, is this where he lives?' she asks.

You've always got to be careful, for people you don't know don't go climbing up five flights of stairs to bring you honours and do you favours. So I play dumb.

'Who?' I ask.

'Monsieur Abdou.'

I think about this for a bit. It could well be a social worker in disguise, so I have to gain some time.

'Don't know any Monsieur Abdou.'

I want to close the door again.

'Wait, little one,' she says.

'What else do you want?'

In the time that it takes her to answer, M'am shows up with her hair all sticky, uncombed, and flour all over her hands. She asks:

'Who is it, Loukoum?'

'Dunno,' I answer.

M'am looks at the tart as if she were a heap of rubbish. Then she smiles and says:

'I've already given New Year's gifts to everyone.'

She slams the door and leans her back against it as she lets out a 'Phew!'

The doorbell rings again.

M'am opens the door. She's furious.

'Really! I've told you that I've already given ... Go away now ... I've a ton of stuff to do with the holidays coming ...'

'I don't need much of your time,' goes the tart. 'I just want to see Monsieur Abdou.'

'Come back some other day. He isn't in.'

But the tart insists. She's like a pot of glue. She says:

'I entrusted my son to your husband ten years ago. My name is Aminata Kouradiom.'

I almost fall over from the blow. I clench my fist very hard. Finally, my hands hurt, so I let my arms hang down. I can't let the words I have in my heart out of my mouth. M'am looks at her without saying a word, as if someone had just cut off her tongue. And her stomach doesn't stop going *gloo-gloc*. She doesn't even think of excusing herself, so overcome is she. Finally, she runs her hands through her hair to straighten it out and puts flour everywhere. You'd think she was an old madwoman of Mali. She says:

'Come in, come in . . .'

The tart comes in, her hands in her pockets. Now her face has got some of its colour back. It's black, as black as M'am is under her layer of powder. And the blush on her cheeks is very flashy. She looks around with shining eyes and a big flat nose. She really looks the house over from top to toe and clucks:

'Well now, this isn't exactly a palace!'

◆

M'am went to wash. She tried to dress like a real white woman, only it's all second-hand clothes. She unearthed a starched and ironed dress, and a white handkerchief. Then she smiles at the tart and asks:

'What can I do for you?'

'Madame, I am a very unhappy woman.'

'So who isn't?' M'am says, looking up to the heavens. 'We all are.'

'Madame, I entrusted my son to your husband ten years ago. For ten years, I've tried to manage as best I could after the great misfortune.'

'And your son, what's his name?'

'Mamadou . . . Mamadou Traoré.'

I'm trembling inside. I feel nothing . . . I even think that I've died.

'And your son's date of birth, when is that?'

The tart's mouth is trembling. Her jaw sags. A tear comes out of her eyes.

'Madame, if you only knew the tragedy young girls in Africa live through. I couldn't do anything else. Today I want to see my son again, ask him to forgive me.'

Then she looks up at me as if she were searching for something she's lost. Then she says:

'I can't live without him.'

'Of course you can't do without him. That doesn't alter the fact that Mamadou brought you a house my husband had built and no less than two thousand French francs. To live off like a queen.'

The tart lets out a cry and begins to blubber like a negress in

86

mourning. M'am sniggers. I've never seen her snigger like that before. It makes my blood run cold.

'Other than that, Mademoiselle, how's business?'

'Oh, all right,' says the tart. 'I get by and I work, it'll take some time, since I've only just started. I haven't yet got the hang of it, as they say.'

'You're on the streets, if I'm not mistaken? Congratulations.'

'Thank you, Madame. I'm also a singer.'

Then she rummages in her bag and pulls out a piece of red cardboard. I'm dying to see what's on it. So I come closer and twist my neck. It shows Aminata next to a piano, with one hand on her hip. She's wearing a huge blonde wig. Her mouth is wide open, you can see all her teeth. She doesn't seem worked up or anything. On the paper it says:

SATURDAY, THE 2ND, COME ONE COME ALL TO HEAR
THE NEW QUEEN OF MALIAN SONG . . .
AND HER LEGENDARY HIP SWAYING.
COME ONE COME ALL.

Allah! That can't *possibly* be my mum. I don't feel like singing about mothers full of grace, holy shit . . . No, this woman just cannot be my gentle mum, this slut who shows her tits like that . . . No . . .

'And now I want to take my son back.'

'Whoa there, not so fast,' M'am says. 'For years and years there's no sign of life . . .'

'Sign of life, sign of life, you must be kidding!'

'That's the last thing I'd do, Mademoiselle. You abandoned your son ten years ago like an old rag. And then one morning you suddenly appear and, just like that, we've got to give him back. It's not that simple, Mademoiselle! This is a home, if you see what I'm talking about . . .'

'I can pay . . .'

And she begins to rummage in her handbag.

'It's not a question of money, Mademoiselle,' M'am says. Then she looks off into nowhere as if it wasn't anything at all.

'Madame, I don't know why you're taking that tone with me. I don't like it at all! I entrusted my son to your husband ten years ago, with the written promise that he would give him back to me as soon as possible. Today, I'm coming to get my son back, and that's my right.'

'Right has nothing to do with it, Mademoiselle, I swear in the name of Allah. There are only duties and you can't say you fulfil yours.'

'We have an agreement on paper.'

'To me, papers that prove things are meaningless. I don't get involved with them. Wait for my husband and you can talk. Would you like something?'

'Some scotch, please.'

'Not allowed, Mademoiselle. But a nice cup of tea from our country, there's nothing better to put you back on your feet.'

M'am smiles and gets up. A few minutes later she comes back with hot tea. The tart drinks, puts down her cup, and says:

'Thank you, Madame, you're very kind.'

'You're welcome, I like to be of use. In whatever way I can.'

'And yet you told Abdou not to marry me.'

'I didn't tell him that.'

'Don't lie.'

'OK then, I didn't really think he shouldn't have.'

'Then why did you say that to him?' she asks M'am, looking her straight in the eyes.

'Because I'm a dummy. Because at the time I was jealous of you and you were doing all sorts of things I can't manage to do.'

'What's that supposed to mean?'

'You gave him a son, that's all.'

And then they stay there just looking at each other, then they lower their heads.

'But I certainly have been punished,' M'am says. 'It changed nothing at all, on the contrary. Now he's really mean.'

'The good Lord doesn't like us to be mean.'

And at that point their little talk takes a whole different turn.

'You did me a great favour, actually,' the creature says.

'How so?'

'I didn't love Abdou, really. It was just for fun, if you see what I mean.'

'Well, at the time Abdou really was something else.'

'We screwed a helluva lot, even while he was married to you. Do you hold that against me?'

'No matter what, if it hadn't been you it would've been someone else, but looking at you, I do wonder why.'

'You don't think I'm attractive?'

'Doesn't matter, now, does it?' M'am says.

'In any case, I had one great love.'

'Oh yes?'

'It was the husband of one of my schoolmates. Bintou was her name. She had big black eyes and skin the colour of the midnight sky. Sometimes I wonder why I hurt her so badly. Not even married three months when I took her man away. There were times when I wouldn't let Fall – that was his name – go home for weeks on end. But when Bintou started having children, he stopped it completely because of his work where everybody was gossiping about it. And his boss, white and Catholic, didn't go for that.

'One day, he came to explain to me how he had to stop seeing me since he wasn't about to lose everything just because of a woman. I tried everything I could to keep him. It didn't work. You see how I have been punished as well. All I want now is for God to forgive me and let me have my son back.'

She turns towards me and asks:

'Is that him?'

And without waiting for M'am to answer she jumps on me. A real frenzy. She kisses me so hard, holds me in such a violent embrace, that I lose my balance. Then she says:

'I recognised him right away, as soon as I saw him. The spitting image of my dad and of me, too. My heart jumped inside my chest. It's the natural law, the law of the blood. Nobody can go against that, not even God himself. Oh, you have no idea what it was like expecting him, waiting and growing bigger and bigger, and then the vomiting and all that. I would touch my belly all the time to see if he was doing all right. When he was born and Abdou took him away . . .'

'Which suited you just fine,' says M'am.

'Oh no, no, not at all!'

There she stands, crying all over again.

'I prayed every single day,' the creature says.

'You must be one of the chosen, seeing that the good Lord listens to you in spite of everything.'

'There, there,' the creature says, 'I'm a decent woman, really I am!'

'I didn't say you weren't.'

'It was in Dakar that the good Lord showed me how much he loved me. He put Amy on my path, one of Abdou's sisters, maybe you know her? She's the one who gave me your address.'

'He could have spared me that!' M'am murmurs between her teeth.

'What'd you say?'

'Nothing.'

In the end, I managed to get out of her grasp. I didn't want to hear any more of what they had to say. I didn't even know any more what was going on. It's true that at first I really wanted to see my mum's face, but now I just don't know any more. I looked in a mirror. I don't know what face to make. It's moments like these that make you really believe it isn't man who created the world. I really wonder if all these women with their talk about God all the time, and about love, and sacrifice, if they have ever really thought about what it is they're saying.

Oh my friend, disaster has rung my doorbell.

The women have gutted themselves behind my back. They've taken off their pagnes and dressed themselves anew in muslin. They've removed the hair from under their armpits and shaved the pubic area. Nothing is called by its name any more. I no longer recognise the geography of the land drawn in MY OWN HOUSE. The pity of it all ... Leave the buttocks as they are, strong and muscular. Let the flesh flow over, they're fat but not ugly at all. Dye the hairs with clay, but let the sexual organs live freely and the sun, reflecting itself there, will indicate the seasons to me.

And they take the initiative. They make love to me and I'm ashamed. They're impaling this little tortured body with love and pleasure. Since when, friend, and in what country do women govern? I am a fertile field, am I not, friend? There's no doubt about the appearance of things, that is to say, my sexual organs, is there now, friend?

Nostalgia exhausts me and tears me apart. When I speak of that place down there, of my country hidden deep inside my inner regions, when I go backwards, I become an embarrassment, a blind thing that understands nothing at all. The women think that I've gone mad. Maybe I am crazy. Threatened, humiliated, ridiculed, I must not proclaim my bad temper.

Tell me, friend, explain it to me. Tell me, you whose intemperate spouse opens herself up to the furious desire to live her own life,

Tell me, you who sublimate the continents of her madness, to the point where the cry of doubt is forgotten,

Tell me if the plucked legs, the shaved sexual parts are those of a woman or a man.

And you, what has become of you?

Me, I am lost.

(Abdou Traoré)

My dad saw Mademoiselle Aminata (I can't bring myself to call her mum). They talked for a long time. When she left, my dad said:

'Life changes, my son. Now that your mother has come back, she'll come to see you often.'

'Yes, dad,' I answered like a well-brought-up child.

I have lots of questions that I'm dying to ask. For example, why didn't he write to her? Why did he lie to me? But nobody asked me anything, so I shut my trap.

My dad also said:

'She's suffered a lot, you know. Try to be nice to her.'

At which point M'am laughed and laughed. My dad bit off a piece of colanut, chewed it, and asked:

'What are you laughing like a fool for?'

◆

Soumana is still sick, sick like I've never seen anyone be sick before. She's having a hard time breathing, it rattles. She no longer gets up. Sometimes dad goes into the bedroom and stays with her. He holds her hand. She pulls loose and says, more like a grumble:

'Will you let go of me or not? Things not going well? I need nobody now!'

On her bed, you'd think they'd put rice powder on her. Her big eyes are shining with fever. And the air is bad. From time to time she opens her eyes, sees my dad and says:

'I don't feel like smelling your filthy cola smell.'

But it's enough to keep my dad from getting close to her any more. He stays in an easy chair in front of the television.

Since Soumana's illness, Madame Saddock comes, whistles, but nobody leans out of the window any more to give her a signal. So she stays there, prowling around the house like a thief. I really wonder what she's looking for.

The whole black tribe has come to pay Soumana a visit. Monsieur Guillaume, Monsieur Kaba, Mademoiselle Esther, Monsieur Ndongala, Monsieur Makossa. They've brought biscuits, cake, and toys for the children, too. Grandmother Kâ Balbine actually came out just to see Sou. She's not a real grandmother, of course. But she's old, older

92

than all of us. She's very well respected because she wears dentures and she speaks a language no one understands.

My aunt Mathilda arrived, dressed up to the nines. M'am is preparing fried plantains with peanut sauce. She takes the skins off the plantains, slices them into small pieces and turns to my aunt Mathilda and asks:

'How's life with you, woman?'

'It'll do,' answers my aunt.

'And Kouam?'

My aunt Mathilda sighs:

'He's working like a dog, for now anyway. But who knows?'

'*Inch Allah!*' M'am says. 'Long may it last.'

'I don't give a shit!' says my aunt Mathilda.

'He is your husband.'

'He's the millstone around my neck,' says my aunt. 'A husband he's not!'

My sisters show up at that moment, yelling:

'We want some broth.'

M'am serves the children. She takes the plantains off the heat, then the two women sit down in the living room. As for me, I keep my ears open to catch what they're saying.

'Kouam is getting on my nerves,' says my aunt Mathilda. 'He thinks I'm his slave.'

'He is your husband. In the Koran it is written that you shall respect your husband always; you shall watch over him to make him a man.'

'There are plenty of divorced women out there who manage very nicely. And besides . . . After what happened at the co nmissioner's, I can't bring myself to forgive him.'

'I'm listening. What happened?'

My aunt Mathilda sniffles and lowers her head, as if the fault were hers.

'If you're not going to tell me, then just go ahead and confess to the good Lord,' M'am says.

'Well, the commissioner asked me to make love to him to set the others free.'

'So?'

'What would you have done in my place?'

M'am sighs deeply and says:

'Makes no difference, 'cause Kouam, he loves you.'

'What about my opinion?'

'Doesn't count,' M'am says.

'And pleasure?'

'What pleasure?' M'am asks.

'Well, when Abdou does it with you, you do feel something, don't you?'

'Sometimes yes, sometimes no. Me, I'm more like his sister now, or even his mother, if you like.'

'Well, I cannot come round to thinking of myself as Kouam's sister, much less as his mother! And when he feels me up, all I want to do is yawn.'

'That's habit,' M'am goes. 'Be patient. It'll come back.'

'Don't think so.'

'Why not?'

'Because when you have a wound you really need to feel it's there so you can take care of it. Seems to me that Kouam doesn't give a shit. He only wants the good part and wants it all for himself.'

'So what are you going to do?'

'Don't know. Maybe I'll just leave him.'

They saw me. Then they lowered their voices.

'Unless I find myself someone else to do it with,' goes my aunt Mathilda.

I understand perfectly well what they want, these chicks, and I don't really understand why men don't want to give them what they want. Too bad! When I understand it all, I'll write to you.

◆

For Christmas, M'am prepared cakes, pancakes, mutton slices. She started very early in the morning. She said:

'There'll be a lot of visitors today!'

All day long she was at the stove. And while she was cooking, she was muttering, talking to herself. When people asked her a question, she'd throw her arms in the air like this; I wonder if she's beginning to go a little bit crazy.

In the afternoon, Aminata arrived all dolled up. She's wearing a red dress with flowers and a black felt hat. She's shining like a well-polished piece of furniture, her frizzy hair is gathered in a bun on top of her head. As appetising as good palm wine. Father thought so too, seeing that he chewed his cola, spat it out, and said: '*Kaie! Kaie!*' which is one of our exclamations.

But she pretended he wasn't there. She came straight over to me, she hugged me. She began to stroke me with her maternal caresses. She touched my hair, fiddled with my ears, let her arms hang over my shoulders and her palms brushed against my chest. Then she grabbed my left hand, examined every finger. I really tried to pull away from her, but she wouldn't hear of it. She kissed each finger, then looked at me as if she'd just seen the Virgin Mary and asked:

'Darling, would you like to go and see Santa Claus today?'

'Don't call me darling, OK?' I said.

Then she didn't say anything more. She looked at my dad. My dad looked at her. They kept looking at each other. Didn't move, didn't talk. For minutes on end. So I took a pancake and spent time in the kitchen. When I came back, I thought they were still there. But no! Aminata was in the toilet, and dad was busy putting on his raincoat.

'Get ready children; we're all going to see Santa Claus.'

'Since when?' M'am asks.

'Since when what?' my dad asks in return.

'Since when are you interested in entertaining the children, Abdou?'

'What're you trying to say? Are you saying I'm not a good father?'

'I didn't say a word!' M'am goes.

'You did, too,' goes my sister, Fatima.

'Mind your own business,' my dad said. But she wouldn't hear of it.

'Hurry up,' he went. 'Go and get ready, quickly. You're going to make everybody late.'

'Oh grown-ups! Oh grown-ups!' she said at last.

Outside it is cold. Just horribly cold. Winter really should try to warm itself nicely in front of the fireplace! There are lots of Santa Clauses on the streets of Paris. Even his own mother would have a hard time telling who he is in this crowd. They all look exactly alike. We went to see the one in the Samaritaine department store. He has a white beard and his big red gown, just for the pleasure of it, and his sled with garlands all around it. There are green trees, pine trees decorated and lit up. There are clowns. They're pretty funny with their coloured faces. I'd really like to watch for a bit longer, but my dad pulled me by my jacket and we went off to see Santa Claus. There are parents with kids dressed like princes. There is a fat lady with a kid who doesn't stop jumping up like a puppydog, and who repeats over and over again: 'I want! I want! I want!' Nobody can possibly tell what it is he wants. Then came my turn. Santa Claus asked:

'What would you like to have, my child?'

'Dunno,' I answered.

'A jet plane, how about that?'

'I dunno,' I answered.

'Maybe an electric car?'

'I dunno.'

Santa Claus scratches his beard like this and says:

'An electric train with a station and a stationmaster, a cowboy, the works, would you like that, my child?'

'Maybe, but I'd like a little happiness,' I tell him. 'Can't you bring me that?'

'Of course, my child,' says he.

Then he takes me in his arms and something goes *pop!* It's a man who has just taken a picture. He turns to my dad and says:

'That will be forty-five francs, sir.'

Now it's Fatima's turn. She climbs on to the platform. She looks Santa Claus straight in the eyes and asks:

'Are you sure you're not here just to cheat the parents?'

'No, my child.'

'Did you come from heaven?'

'Yes, my child.'

'Is it really God who sends you?'

'Yes, my child.'

'Then why aren't you African?'

'That's fate, my child.'

'Not true! You see, you're lying just to cheat the parents. You're not African 'cause you're not Santa Claus.'

'She's right,' goes the woman whose kid kept saying 'I want! I want!'

'Our ancestors were black. I read it in the newspaper, the first Eve was black.'

'If that's how it is . . .' a man in a hat said. And he took his son's hand and walked off. The other parents followed suit.

I don't know who that Eve woman is, but I can assure you that's the biggest lie I ever heard in my entire life.

◆

This evening, there's quite a crowd at home. They're happy. They think the trees, the flowers, the earth, all belong to them. And the stars as well. They're all sitting on the floor like at a picnic. They're playing cards, others are playing lido. They're talking about all sorts of things, but me, I'm thinking about Lolita and wondering how white people celebrate the New Year. At last, my dad takes out his tape recorder and puts on some cassettes, music from Mali. It's loud enough to wake up the dead.

'Let the party begin!' he says.

Everyone applauds and people are beginning to dance. But there's Madame Zola, our neighbour, arriving. She knocks. She says the music is bothering her, that she can't sleep. But she doesn't look like someone who's trying to sleep, seeing that she is wearing a grey dress and the four hairs on her head have just come out of their rollers. She doesn't mean any harm, Madame Zola. But it can't always be fun to live alone with an autistic child as your only companion.

'Come in, come in, Madame Zola,' says father opening the door wide.

She refuses at first, out of politeness. M'am looks at her, her eyes say: 'Come in, come in, M'am will put you back on your feet.' And my dad insists. Finally she accepts. She comes into the room. Monsieur Kaba invites her to dance and they dance. After that, Madame Zola is right in the mood.

'It's been years since I've danced,' she says with a laugh.

'Make the most of it, Madame,' goes Monsieur Kaba. 'Besides, you're an excellent partner.'

All this is nothing but niceties, but Madame Zola smiles with pleasure and her cheeks go as red as tomatoes.

So, I watch all this absentmindedly. But suddenly something happens. Someone is knocking at the door. And the tart (sorry, my mum) makes an entrance nobody could miss.

She's not alone. A gentleman accompanies her. Very well dressed, with a black suit, white shirt, and a tie. I don't know him. But he is black and welcome in the tribe. She, on the other hand, I swear to you she's shining like the sun. She's wearing a little dress with diamonds held up by tiny straps. You almost see the tips of her breasts. And everybody is waiting for it to slide down. But it holds up nicely. As for me, I can hardly believe my eyes. Seeing her like that, you'd never know she had a kid my age.

'Help!' cries Monsieur Richard. 'I feel horny!'

Then he approaches Aminata:

'I'm at your beck and call,' he says to her.

'I don't ask for that much,' she answers. 'Just a scotch and some ice.'

'And you, sir?' he asks the unknown man.

'Same for me.'

Then my aunt Mathilda comes closer too, the eternal cigarette butt in her mouth.

'How lovely you are, my dear!' And she looks at her as if she were about to give herself a treat. And it really strikes me, the way she is looking at her. Not like a woman. But like a man. Because women always watch each other with a bit of jealousy, never any tenderness, and even less so looking as if they were about to treat themselves to something nice. Besides, they never say: 'How lovely you are, my dear!' in that way.

In the room, every man is watching Aminata. They're watching only her, it's as if the others weren't even there.

The man who's with Aminata takes her hand, looks her in the eyes and says: 'It's certainly true, you are exquisite, my dear!'

At that moment, my dad leaps up like a fury. He comes right to her and looks at her as if she were a ghost.

'May I introduce Monsieur Nkomo,' she says to him.

'What's wrong with you, dressing up like a whore?' my dad asks.

'None of your business,' she answers.

'You have to behave like a responsible woman,' he retorts.

'The way I dress certainly pleases my man, doesn't it, darling?' she asks Monsieur Nkomo.

'Your scenes aren't mine,' Monsieur Nkomo says. 'I'm all for peace, not war.'

'Take that off immediately,' my dad orders the creature.

'Don't overdo it, Abdou. I'm not your wife.'

'But you are the mother of my son.'

'Won't stop me, right, son?' she asks me.

Me, I pretend I haven't heard a thing and say:

'You'd be better off dancing.'

'Out of the mouths of babes,' says my dad.

And he pulls her along. Off they've gone to sway to the rhythm of the music that's beating away.

It is then that Soumana drags herself in. Sick as a dog. She is dressed like a true African queen. She is wearing a very fancy *boubou*, blue with gold all around the chest and the sleeves. A scarf with diamonds and red fringes falls down over her cheeks. She is also carrying a snakeskin handbag and wearing sandals that match. She is really elegant, like I've never seen before. She's edging her way through, wobbling between the dancers. And several times she almost falls because she is struggling to stay on her feet. The yellow powder on her face is like plaster, but it doesn't matter much, seeing that she's giving it her all and that's always a pleasure in cases like this. She plants herself in front of the couple and asks:

'May I dance with my man?'

'After this dance,' my dad answers.

'Right now!' Soumana orders.

'Allah Kabia!' M'am says because she smells trouble.

But my dad doesn't listen. He continues dancing. And then Soumana puts her hands on her hips and screams:

'I'm not dead yet! I'm not dead yet. She's not going to do this to me while I'm still alive.'

'She's in the same position as you are where I'm concerned,' says my dad.

'Don't insult me, Abdou,' she shrieks. 'That one, she's nothing but a hussy.'

Aminata says: 'Excuse me.'

'And high time, too,' answers Soumana. 'You slut!'

You can see Aminata is beginning to have enough of this; she says again: 'Excuse me.'

'Out! Dirty whore!' Soumana screams and shoves a fist in her face.

At that point Aminata sees red. She turns around, she raises her hand. But my dad has enough time to see it coming. He grabs Aminata's hand. 'Don't do it,' he says again and again as if in prayer, 'don't do it.' And he holds on to her hand and they stand there looking at each other, just like that, as if there were no one else around, while Soumana keeps on yelling: 'Whore! Whore! Whore!'

Finally, Aminata calms down, she goes looking for her banker and they leave without saying goodbye to anyone. Dad takes Soumana by the shoulders to help keep her upright. But he cannot manage it by himself because of her weight. Monsieur Makossa runs over and helps him to walk Soumana to her room. African solidarity is really great, don't you think?

Then everybody began to talk. Especially Monsieur Makossa. He says:

'It always turns sour when you mix different types. After all, we're not of the same class, are we?'

Everyone grunts. Then Monsieur Makossa explains that he knows Aminata's escort. A lout! Depraved! How do you think he had that fine suit made on a banking salary? By selling his arse, of course! And he's even heavily involved in money-laundering! A bastard! A swine! Aaaah! When people still had all their wits about them, they would never have eaten at the same table as this crook! This body-snatcher ... And then, to cap it all, this bandit wants to marry the daughter of a chief of State ... Yes, didn't you know? Absolutely. He stood for election to be president of something or other, but he only got one vote, his own! The people aren't that moronic! They'd never accept a faggot ...

But as for me, I can tell you that I've nothing against faggots, because they have everybody's clear conscience against them. But to offer your arse, you really have to like it otherwise it's pretty repulsive, because after all selling your arse is really a chick's job.

My dad came back into the living room, looking perfectly happy. He asked:

'Everything all right, friends?'

'Yeah!' everyone answered, laughing.

'Fine,' he said, 'let the party continue!'

I know it was only to have the good mood take over, for without that you're nowhere.

Madame Zola went over to father and said:

'Your evening is a real success, Monsieur Abdou, but I really must go . . .'

'Oh, stay a little longer,' my dad insisted. 'The party is just getting started. Come on, dance with me.'

She accepted gladly. She was moving her behind as in a sex-shop with a little teasing smile. Giggling, she was saying how it reminded her of her youth, when she could still use both her feet and could climb up the stairs ten times without getting tired. What happened after that I don't know any more, and when I woke up in the morning, there were empty bottles everywhere and leftovers in the dish.

Timothée came and knocked on the door. I opened it and asked him if he wanted to taste some of the left-overs. He said he did. I gave them to him and he ate. That same evening he had hives. He was scratching everywhere. That's how we celebrated Christmas Eve.

In my House, the giraffe of anguish is whirling around.

Upright on top of a woman, I've seen the night arrive.
Dreams of premonition were piling up on the horizon.
I've lost the legend, I didn't know how to decode it.
Life obliterates our tracks when we dream too much.
I no longer know who I am. Exploded barrier.
The dawn of perdition is bathing my house in a wounding light.
I give you the key to my truth. I want to forget time that bleeds and arches. I still want to believe in the sweetness of the fertile earth.
You know, before, my voice would sing beautifully.
Womankind would adorn herself in love,
She would abolish emptiness, and without hesitation she would make the springs of hope flow.

Woman has changed. I see theories come down the staircase of reason, bring wind to turn the past into echoing monuments. Who then inhabits these theories? Woman is equal to man! Yet I know that when she is strong, she is the earth's grimace. Weak, she gives drink from the bottom of despair.

My destiny is toppling. I'm not telling you anything else. Days that mark their dreariness. Sad. Flat. Without surprise. I'm always astonished at how small I am. Not even any sex since the women weigh down upon my shoulders and shit on my head. Every day I dig a little more deeply into the shadow in search of a flame. Of a scrap of understanding.

Why? I've done what was necessary. I sold my life to work for a little bit of bread, so that the brightness of woman's eyes would be full of affection.

From this coffin, my House, I demand only laughter, the drunkenness of dance. And tenderness placed there as a well-deserved reward.

102

Why? One of them daubed herself with lipstick, the other painted her eyes like two enormous black holes. I no longer recognise them. What is happening? Nothing has a name any longer! I don't know anything any more. I am nothing any more. And every day, the women hack away a little at my dreams, these dreams constructed for them. I am afraid. And instead of telling you, explaining to you the reasons why it is absolutely necessary for a man to have two wives, I am boring you with my anguish.

Even my innermost regions are becoming weary. Exhausted, tired out by my never-ending questions.

(Abdou Traoré)

During the holidays, I play with my friend Alexis. But it's cold outside, really cold. We played soccer, and pinball, but Monsieur Ndongala wasn't there to give us any more money to play with, nobody has seen him since Christmas night, even father is worried. M'am said that he must have found a place to hang out, of course, where he can eat and take a nap. And everybody thought that was very funny, except for me, of course, but that's life!

One day Alexis stole some change. But Monsieur Guillaume noticed it. He really let him have it and then grounded him. The day seemed very long to me, long like it was in Africa, so then I wandered around without really knowing where I was heading, all the way to Lolita's building. First I took rue Jean-Pierre Timbaud, then I continued on the boulevard de Belleville, and then the rue de Belleville.

There I ran into Madame Saddock. She was wearing a black coat, gloves, and a felt hat. I lowered my head so that she wouldn't see me. But she had. She called me:

'Loukoum! Loukoum . . .'

She caught up with me.

'How are things going, my boy?'

'Fine,' I answered because I wasn't in the mood.

'And M'am, how's she? And Sou?'

'Very well, very well,' I said.

'Ah,' she goes. 'That's odd. I've been trying for several days now to see them, but no one answers. I don't understand.'

'They don't want to speak to you, Madame.'

'Why not?' she asks baffled. 'What's happened?'

'I don't know, Madame. I don't understand anything about grown-ups' business.'

She smiled in a strange way, but I knew it wasn't a real smile, seeing there wasn't anything to smile about.

'Would you like to come with me for some ice-cream, Loukoum?'

'Yeah,' I went.

I don't like that woman, but I love strawberry ice-cream. .

So we went to a café. Madame Saddock ordered tea and while I was at it I had four scoops of strawberry ice-cream. I really had a feast. But her, she wouldn't stop talking, asking questions. It was obvious she wanted to pump me. But I wasn't born yesterday! All she has to do is go see Inspector Malcom if she wants more information.

I wolfed down my ice-cream and got away from her so quickly I even forgot to say thank you.

I went back up the rue de Belleville. It was raining . . .

It was raining on my head and the wind was making circles of rain on the pavement and blowing into my jacket.

A car came by, the tyres screeched, it almost had an accident on the boulevard de Belleville. Somewhere a door slammed. Somebody shouted something.

It was raining hard. Just as in the stories M'am tells me. Rain is the spirit of good, it helps children grow, a little like the milk you suckle! Sometimes I really think the rain is my mum's milk, the one I don't know. I open my mouth and let the water flow in, and I am as happy as can be . . . Because it's the spirit of the ancestors I'm drinking and this way I won't lose my identity completely. I don't tell this to anyone, though, because white people don't believe in stories like these.

Finally I made it to Lolita's house. Inside their flats, people were watching television. Some of them had decorated their places with metallic garlands all around their windows. I stopped in front of the block of flats. The front door was open. I stayed outside with my wet jacket. And I watched. A gentleman went into the building with flowers. An old lady came out with a nylon scarf on her head to keep her hair from being soaked. I just kept watching. A dog and a cat came by. They were both running. The dog was walking as if on the diagonal because he was cold. I called him but he didn't answer. He went off to hide under a tree and was watching me. And me, I thought of the homeless of Belleville who are all alone without a roof over their head for protection.

'What the hell are you doing there?'

I turn around.

It's an old lady. She is wearing a grey raincoat with buttons like pine trees.

'There's no prohibition against being outside,' I told her.

'Where do you live?'

'None of your business,' I answered.

'Oh! Really now!' she went, as if in shock. 'The kids today, really! When I was young!'

'*Inch Allah*, Madame.'

'What nerve!' she said.

'*Inch Allah!*'

She mumbled something. She shook her head. Then she left. I looked at every window of Lolita's house. I said to myself that perhaps she was really looking at me at the same time, but I didn't see her, but I knew she was there because there were flowers in the windows. And then I stayed anyway.

That's when I heard a voice:

'What're you doing here, Mamadou?'

It was Lolita. She was with a woman. They were carrying packages. I came to the conclusion they'd been shopping.

'You know him?' the lady asks.

'Of course,' she goes. 'He's in my class.'

They come closer. They look exactly alike. The mother is very skinny. She has a pile of hair on her head.

'What're you doing there in the rain, little guy? You're going to end up catching your death of cold! Come on in . . .'

We went up to Lolita's place. I took off my jacket and hung it neatly in the wardrobe. Honestly, Lolita's house is the most beautiful house I've ever seen! There's a room that's bigger than our entire house, a kitchen, two bathrooms, and then bedrooms. Lolita's mother gave me a towel to dry my hair. Then she served us biscuits and milk. It was better than at my house, I don't know why.

'Do you live in the neighbourhood?' Lolita's mother asked.

'No, a bit further down,' I answered. 'I'm from Mali.'

'You really shouldn't wander around in the rain,' she went again.

I said nothing.

'Do you live with your parents?'

'Yeah.'

'What does your father do?'

I explained what he did. She listened reverently. White people listen to black people when you tell them your woes. But when you tell them that all is well, that you don't need them, then they don't listen any more.

Well, I wasn't going to do her that favour and tell her that my dad has two wives and lots of mistresses, that my mother is a whore. No, I told her a story white people don't like to hear. That we were well off. That my dad works in the mayor's office. That my mum is a cashier at Ed's.

She yawned. She said:

'Go and play in your room. Don't make too much noise.'

Lolita had a room all to herself with white curtains and a beautiful bedspread with birds of paradise on which I didn't dare sit.

First we played with a puzzle. Then we played mummies and daddies, the game I like best.

'Show me,' she suddenly said.

'Show you what?' I asked.

'Your willy, of course! You never showed that to a girl before, I bet.'

'Of course I have,' I lied.

'So why not show it now?'

'I just don't want to, that's all.'

'Then you're a sad case! You're still a virgin.'

'Not at all,' I said.

'Well then, show it.'

'You first.'

'If you want. Go and watch the door, just in case.'

'Right,' I said.

She sniggers. She lies down on the bed. She lifts up her dress. She pulls down her panties. Pooh, it's like a heart, like you see in natural

106

science lessons. No hair around it, like on Soumana's thing. But inside, it looks like a moistened rose.

'Is it pretty?' she asks.

I come closer, look at it, touch her little bud that's all pink and feel a light tickling inside my belly. Something like a shiver. Oh, no big deal, but enough for me to be aware of. Next time I'll fiddle with it a bit longer.

'Is it pretty?' she asks again.

'Dunno.'

That's when she gets up. She comes over to me and says:

'Your turn.'

'No.'

'You promised.'

'No,' I said. 'There's a place in the Koran where it says that it's bad.'

'It's your own good Lord who made it, isn't it? So then it has to be good.'

And there she goes, throwing herself on me, grabbing my trousers and pulling at the zip. I can't move, it's as if I'm paralysed on the inside. A whole flock of birds is singing inside my head. Wind is blowing. Trees are swaying. Not that they're far from me. A feeling of being part of all that. For example, if the tree should fall, I'll fall with it. It's really weird.

Lolita clucks.

'Honestly, you, you really are gross,' she says as she looks at my pecker, as if she can't believe her eyes.

I look down at my dick. It's standing straight up. I'm thinking about the times that M'am used to wash me. And how that, too, would give me a little shudder. Sometimes, a big shudder.

'There's my mum!' she yelled.

I quickly pulled up my underwear and my trousers. I had the impression we'd done something that wasn't right.

'I have to go now,' I said.

Then I looked at her and added:

'We shouldn't do that again, or else the good Lord is not going to be pleased with us.'

But sometimes, in the middle of the night, when I hear noises coming from my parents' bed, I pull the blanket over my head and I play with my pecker and I think about Lolita and it stands straight up again.

What is to be done, friend? To make an imaginary temple out of nothingness, one that cannot die. Woman has changed. She has changed her pagne *for trousers. Listen to me once again.*

Listen to my fears sewn together by the nights.

Images come and go. Words of the past. Drumming. I have to let myself go off into reveries in order not to spit up my rage.

In former times, down there in my country?

Listen.

My eyes are shut and behind my closed eyelids there is a woman's gaze that shines more brightly than the sun. From head to toe, she is like ebony. Her cheeks are like heaven and her waist like an ear of corn. Nightly, on her shoulders, there are two silver braids whose ends are finished off with rings of gold.

Behind my closed eyelids, there is an extinguished face, a wound, an injury, a silhouette filled with forests and words fleeing from me.

I feel her present in front of me, standing there like a gift from nature. Her name is Star.

She holds out her naked and strong arms to me. She calls me, she calls out to me. She claims that she is able to put me at the threshold of paradise. A death as sweet as that of the birds who are lost in the sky. She pulls me toward her, she ensnares me. How do I resist, friend, tell me? How does one entrust one's soul to a woman?

Her eyes are a heaven of eternity, populated with diamonds. How can I resist, friend? Don't say anything. You, too, must know nighttime dreams like these which grow pale as the day begins to dawn. Listen:

The ancients were right to cover their first female child over with earth. They were holding back misfortune.

(Abdou Traoré)

Good Lord! Mademoiselle Esther came to our house. She doesn't look well. She is pale. You'd think she's put rice powder on her face. And she seems a bit doddery. She has bouts of nausea. She drinks tea, vomits, she eats cake, vomits. All she does is vomit.

That's all we need at home, right now. With Soumana who is getting sicker and sicker. She hardly eats any more. M'am wakes up several times a night to check on her breathing.

'What exactly is wrong with her?' I asked.

'It's her chest,' M'am answered me.

M'am seems more and more tired and sad. My dad doesn't get too close any more, because Soumana doesn't want him near. She doesn't even have the strength to say so any longer. All she has are her eyes to express her hostility.

So when Mademoiselle Esther arrived with her share of misery, M'am didn't have the energy to get to work. She said:

'You should see a doctor.'

'I did.'

'And?' M'am asked.

'I'm gonna have a baby.'

It was like a bombshell. My dad spat his cola *splat!* and asked:

'How many months?'

'Almost three.'

'No problem, you can have an abortion.'

'I don't want to.'

'And why not? And first of all, who's the father?'

'What a question!' she said, outraged.

'What do you mean, what a question!' my dad went. 'With girls today, who knows? They open their legs to everyone . . . So you can't swear to anything now, can you?'

'I know perfectly well who made this one,' Mademoiselle Esther said looking my dad straight in the eyes.

'Who?' M'am asked.

'It's his,' she said pointing at my dad.

He didn't answer. He lowered his head.

'How would you know?' M'am snarled.

'I swear to it,' Mademoiselle Esther said.

'And what're you going to do?' M'am asked.

'Dunno.'
Then she added:
'You're there, right, M'am?'
Inch Allah!

Since the women have started serving glasses full of independence in my house, since they've been drinking that sap, I am learning how not to be a man any longer. Who am I? An immigrant. A burdensome mouth. An airstream passing through.

I have no landmark any more. I limp in my infirmity with the shamelessness of a ravaged body.

Tell me, friend, how do you manage? How did you succeed in extricating from your body, from your soul this liberation of your wife's, which chains up your male strength?

Here, we have marabouts. Marabouts whose souls are lost in the twists and turns of civilisation. Their mouths no longer know. Their memories have lost the legend. Their eyes stare at the sky. Obstinately. Torn away from their soil, they have left their knowledge behind.

They talk. They still talk. They people their mouths with legends the end of which they have forgotten. Homesickness forces us to believe. Nostalgia moors us to their lies. What is to be done, friend?

Beliefs do not tolerate exile. They are like trees. Uprooted. Posted. Sent off in the cold of the ship's hold, they lose their foliage. They arrive dried out. Dead.

I no longer know to whom I should turn.

My wives are angry with me. The bodies they offer me no longer jostle each other to give me the joy I lack. Their faces are tortured with rancour, with accumulated hatred. They say: 'Every day you lock us in, and with every day we are free, with every day more dead and still more alive, more wretched and more royal, eternally damned but still under a suspended sentence, absent ones badly released, oppressed, but unique under the highest heavens, we, two women.'

The women have understood nothing at all. Under exile from the sun their skin has cracked. Something has become unhinged. Your

111

wife's theories have infiltrated without their knowledge, behind my
back. They are turning my life into a nightmare. They accuse me
saying: 'You are the executioner of our soul. You think you are
charitable, but you're as cold as the blade of a knife. You don't kill,
but you rob life of every moment.'

And what are they making of the warmth of my hands?

(Abdou Traoré)

Soumana is getting more and more ill. She gets weaker with every passing day. Father has called in a doctor. It must really be serious then, seeing that asking a doctor to come to the house is a luxury only bosses can afford, as if it isn't a shame to be throwing money out the window.

When the doctor saw our house and the kids blubbering all over the place, he cried from behind his big beard:

'It's a proper nursery school here!'

And everyone laughed.

Then he examined Soumana. Ever since I can remember I've never seen Soumana ill. I mean sick in bed. She complains all the time, as you already know, that's what she does. She's constantly got a pain somewhere, in her head, her feet, her back, unless it's my dad she's complaining about with his marital infidelities.

But now, she is really and truly ill. When my dad went into the bedroom, the doctor looked at him and said:

'I can't say what'll happen if you don't take her to the hospital immediately.'

'She doesn't have cancer?' my dad asked.

'No, sir.'

The doctor scratches his beard and adds:

'But it doesn't look very good!'

He's a great doctor. He really knows his stuff. He insists that my dad transfer Soumana to the hospital and that she be given proper care. Soumana says:

'Oh, no, doctor! I don't want to go to the hospital. I don't want to leave my children. I'll get better.'

112

She turned her head, looked at the doctor with a weak little smile, then added:

'If it weren't for my kids, I would have been in the other world a long time ago.'

The doctor nodded. Then he wrote out a prescription. He looked at us. There is sadness in his eyes.

He explains to my dad that Soumana has an illness which is clogging up her veins and the blood cannot circulate where it needs to go. He said something like pulmonary trombolis which I didn't quite get. And that she'd be better off in a large ward with intensive care.

'What do you want, doctor? She refuses. You know what women are like . . . They're all stubborn as mules.'

'As you wish, sir. But if you need anything at all, give me a call.'

'Thank you, thank you, my dear sir.'

My dad flops into his chair. He looks very detached. But I notice he is chewing the ends of his nails. Then he lets out a deep sigh like when the sky is falling down on your head.

I close the door behind the doctor. I go to see Soumana in the corner where her bed is. She is fully stretched out. She takes up the whole of it with one arm here and the other arm on the other side of the bed. She's moaning, she's muttering with pain. I can easily see how she's struggling to breathe. She's all grey and dripping with sweat, like an enormous piece of chocolate melting in the sun. M'am is on her knees at the foot of the bed.

Soumana opens her eyes, turns her head to us, says:

'Stop your little act, M'am. You're pleased, come on now . . . You'll have him all to yourself soon enough, your man. Just like that.'

'Don't say such foolish things, Sou. Women like you never go under.'

'Is it your good Lord who told you that?'

'What if he did?'

'You're a lucky woman to have your good Lord listen to you; as for me, he and I have been divorced for quite a while now.'

'Soumana!' M'am cries out, horrified.

'Oh stop, M'am. Nobody believes in that old man any more, somewhere up there in his cloud of dust. All you have to do is look at yourself and you'll understand what I mean.'

'Sou, listen to me. I know I'm nothing special. I haven't had babies. I'm black, I'm ugly, I'm not even capable of working the whole blessed day behind some desk. But the good Lord does love me and that, nobody can take *that* away from me.'

M'am falls silent, then adds in a dull voice: 'I'm alive and that's enough.'

'Fat lot of good it does you!' Soumana says. 'So why hasn't he given you anything at all, like he did to white women, for instance?'

'Mathilda, you know, isn't any better off than you or me. She has her share of trouble, too.'

'That's not a reason. You pray, all you do is pray, and he sits up there all swollen with pride because all you do is pray to him. Seems to me he's just deaf!'

'Don't talk that way, Sou. If he's listening to you he'll not let you be part of his Koran any more.'

'I don't give a shit! I've nothing to lose, seeing that he's never given me anything.'

'Sou, he gave you life, didn't he, and your children as well, and your mother before you. And then there are lovely things here on earth. Have you ever really looked at the sunset?'

'So what?'

'When you look at the sun and when it gets to be all red and black because it's going down, you feel you're in perfect·harmony with nature, and at that moment you know God loves you.'

'All I know is that whores, forgers, drug addicts, murderers are having a fine old time of it, while the rest of us, we're busy fretting over "Thou shalt not kill, thou shalt honour thy father and thy mother". Me, I know his world is a rotten mess because he is a man!'

'Nobody ever said he was a man. It's the men who invented that one, for their own lavish enjoyment, so they can crush women,' M'am says.

'You think it's a woman?'

'May well be. Only women can give birth to children.'

M'am is marvellous, I tell you. A gigantic rose, you'd say. She glanced at the window before she went on:

'Your son is a man, there's the real drama. They're the ones who take everything away from us, even the will to live, and we're here

114

thinking it's the good Lord who wants to harm us. Do you remember the day Abdou came into your bed?'

'I remember it as if it were yesterday.'

'I was in such pain that night, I cried. I thought I would drown in my tears, Sou. But towards morning, I saw a pigeon on my windowsill. I watched and kept watching it and thought: "How great God is!" And he is great, Sou, since he's given me the joy of children even though I never did give birth.'

At that, Soumana gave a little hiccough, then said:

'He gives me the impression that he doesn't listen to any woman, that he's asleep up there and couldn't care less about us, you know. But still, it's something to think he's around, that he loves us. At least there is someone there we can check with to see whether he loves us. And you think maybe he does. Better that way. Well, let me be now, I want to rest.'

M'am went out of the room. I sat down next to Soumana. She falls asleep and snores like a storm. It's true that I don't like her. But suddenly I realise that she's very important to me. Because of nostalgia. It's true, life is beautiful but you don't find that out till later.

Outside, a car passed by honking its horn, a dog barked, a lady was calling her son: 'Damien! Damien!' Life went on.

Soumana woke up. She looked at me in terror, as if I were a ghost.

'He mustn't take me to the hospital, Loukoum, otherwise they might send me back to Africa.'

'No, Sou,' I said.

'You sure, Loukoum?'

'We're in France, Sou. Nobody can send you where you don't want to go.'

'You're not lying are you, little one?'

'*Inch Allah*, I promise, I swear,' I went.

I took her hand. It was cold and all clammy. I held it tight, very tight.

Then she asked me:

'Why doesn't Madame Saddock come to see me any more?'

'*I* don't know. Maybe she's sick, too, or maybe she found herself a guy, or maybe she doesn't have time. You know what life in Paris is like.'

'Still, it's strange . . .'

Then I said:

'Don't worry, Sou. Me, when I'm big, I'll take you to Cannes. Down there, there's the sea, the sky, forests of mimosas, film stars, English lords, princesses of Monaco who romp around with each other on the beach in their swimsuits. There are balloons that come down from the sky and clowns in the streets. There'll be a producer who'll see you and you'll be an actress.'

I didn't believe a single word of what I was saying, I swear to you! But I didn't see what else I could do, especially with that Madame Saddock business. She smiled. Her smile is enormous, since her face has become so skinny. I've never loved her this much, Allah! I picked up her bag, rummaged through it, found the picture when she was twenty and not yet overweight. Looking at it, I thought how truly beautiful she was, only in the picture she looked yellow. Looking at what she used to be, you never would have imagined that this is what it would come to in the end.

Between you and me, friend, I don't know how you manage with your wife. The story goes that your wife is an easy lay, a pushover as light as a bird's feather. Generous, she distributes long hours of tenderness to passers-by. The story goes that she pleads for liberty and that she makes a scene in front of you with great tantrums and most interesting tears.

And you, friend, you step up your attentions towards her, and out of concern, you worry about every detail so she seems happy and in the end better treated than yourself.

I wonder how you mask your jealousy. Sometimes I encounter your wife, little moon with naked legs, a murmur of love that runs from city to city evoking tenderness. Where are you? Does she carry you within herself? Have you become so light, so light? Or else do you transform yourself into a little bird that sings when she is giving herself to others?

Your understanding escapes me.

What is the moon doing in the field of men, far away from home? What is she doing inside that skirt that unveils her? She crosses the square and struts about. Why is she killing hours and hours behind a desk? She laughs and you, you fall asleep with a smile, and bitterness hidden away in the meanderings of history.

Enveloped in madness, I imagine your jealousy and your grudges, which you must swallow in order not to seem reactionary. I am becoming hard, cutting as the blade of a dagger, but a dagger without a hand to accompany it to the crime. Who, after all, am I? I don't even exist, so . . .

But you know, friend, woman's independence is a bad seed which man must throw in the dustbin. If he misses the first throw, it will fall and grow no matter where. Even between her legs!

(Abdou Traoré)

117

We're back at school. Mademoiselle Garnier is absent. There is a substitute. She's young. Less experienced than Mademoiselle Garnier. So nobody listens to her.

Pierre Pelletier is teaching me history and geography. He explains to me that over there, that's America, where blacks sold other blacks to work in the cottonfields of white people. I don't really understand this business. I've never heard anybody in my family talk about that. Not even Monsieur Ndongala. It seems that we're not responsible. So, these tons of blacks who croaked are none of our business.

Still, I really would like to go to the United States. I'd really like to see that land where so many of our brothers suffered, worked, died in the hope of one day seeing Africa again. I'd really like to kiss that ground, I don't know why. A small thing inside me, like a voice come out of history. I'm not familiar with it. But it's there.

Pierre Pelletier is nice. He also talks about Egypt which is in Africa. He explains that there used to be a civilisation there as great and powerful as western civilisation. He makes me do my maths, and a lot of things to make me become smarter. But with the holidays that went on and on, I have the impression that I don't remember anything. That it's been centuries since I was last in school. That I've forgotten everything. Then I think that my mind is slow, that the message won't go in that deeply. But there are things inside us that we know we know, and I don't need Pierre Pelletier to know that.

The new teacher is really having a hard time. Nobody listens to her. No matter how much she screams, it's as if she were spitting into the ocean. So then she said:

'Today we're going to talk about our Christmas holidays. I'm asking the bravest one to raise his or her hand and start.'

All the kids raised their hands and wouldn't stop yelling: 'Me, Miss! Me, Miss!' Everyone except me, for I have nothing to tell, I thought, so I shoved my hands inside my pockets. I lowered my head.

But the new teacher saw it all. As for me, I looked elsewhere as if nothing were happening. But that woman has the eyes of a black man, I tell you that for a fact. Not of blacks like my dad who cannot see whether a cat is grey or black in the night, but black men from before. Monsieur Ndongala says that in Larousse or something like that which you have to read to be smarter, it says that runaway or fugitive blacks could see the white men who were pursuing them from very far away.

Suddenly, the teacher called out, pointing at me:

'Loukoum, will you please tell us about your Christmas?'

'Me?' I asked in surprise.

'I don't see anyone else,' Alexis said.

I stood up. The whole class is watching me. And me, I am only looking at Lolita. I can see her soft, very, very soft skin very well. Seems to me that her mother must have put a lot of pampers on her for her skin to be so soft.

'We're listening,' says the teacher.

'I'm a Muslim,' I answer.

'That makes no difference,' she says to me. 'Santa Claus can be found in every country.'

'In my religion it is forbidden to talk about infidels,' I answer.

The new teacher shakes her head several times, as if to let something drop. It worked, seeing that she asked me to sit down. Then she said:

'Richard Dellacqua, would you please tell us about your Christmas holiday?'

Richard Dellacqua stood up. He planted himself in front of the new teacher, crossed his arms like a good pupil and spoke:

'First, Mum and Dad got up. They were in their dressing gowns and we had breakfast in the living room. We had toast, jam, butter, scrambled eggs on toast. And me, I don't like scrambled eggs. Mum said: "Eat up! Eat up! You're too skinny." And my dad watched me with eyes like this, and so I ate and ate, then my stomach started going up and down, and up again and down. I ran to the toilet, a nook for solitary needs as my dad always says, I stuck my fingers down my throat and threw up and threw up some more.'

'And then your mother cooked the vomit?' Alex asked.

'Yuk . . . Yuk . . . That's disgusting,' the others shouted.

'Quiet!' the teacher yelled. 'Cross your arms, all of you, on your desks and you, Richard, go on with your story.'

'We had guests for Christmas, aunts and cousins, whom we see once in a blue moon, because in France it's each for himself and God for us all! They're cousins and aunts on my mother's side, I have other cousins, too, girls, on my father's side, but I'd rather not bore you with their problems because they make my aunts' blood boil, who then chew their fingernails hoping that the blood will become pure again. Then, we go to my grandmother Odette's house. She is very old and speaks Flemish, which is the regional language of Fort Mardyck. She calls me "my little darling" because she doesn't like the grown-ups who carry original sin with them and who vote for the left, where they take away from you everything you own and have earned by the sweat of your brow. She ought to be living in a convent to protect herself from the perversities and the degradation of society, at least that's what I think, because she's always saying things like: "Where are we heading? Where's the world going? Oh, Lord, in my day ...!" On my father's side I have no grandfather, I don't know him because he died of a heart attack while watching a match on television "France-England". Since you don't know this, it's a game that comes down hard, as is always the case, on people with a sensitive heart. On my mother's side, I do have a grandfather. He's retired from Renault-Billancourt. Now, he says, his life has changed, he can quietly enjoy a well-deserved rest but he's still always talking about nuts and bolts. He always goes to bed very early and grumbles about his neighbours who make a racket after ten o'clock at night. He yells. I don't get it because he has all day to sleep. If you want my opinion, Grandpa should go to an old-age home to calm his nerves. As far as I'm concerned, I think he should put a personal ad in *Libération*, so he can get married and warm himself, for loneliness is a terrible thing and kills more people than cancer does.

'For Christmas dinner, Odette prepared a turkey with chestnuts, then we went to the Apostolic Catholic Church to thank the good Lord for there not being any head colds in our family, now and forever more, amen.'

Then came Johanne Dégoud's turn.

'City dump!' someone called out.

'Get the broom!' someone else said.

You should understand them and forgive them if possible. Johanne Dégoud is so fat and ugly that even the dogs in France, who piss everywhere, wouldn't dare do it in front of her eyes. They'd be too scared, I guarantee, without meaning any harm. When she looks at you, you'd think it was a ghost, when she doesn't look at you, you'd still think it was a ghost. Still, she talked! That's democracy; what else do you want?

'I like the Christmas holidays because during the break, which is there for the creation of the unverifiable Nativity, as for its veracity . . .'

'Hot air!'

'Oooeeeh!' Alex cried.

'Bor-ing!'

'Quiet!' the teacher shouted.

Nobody was listening to her. Everyone laughed out loud. The teacher was furious. Alex got down on all fours and was laughing like an epileptic horse. The teacher came to grab him by the collar. As for me, I was trying to see what Lolita was up to. She was doing nothing, she wasn't even laughing. It was as if someone had scolded her only no one had. Then the teacher pushed Alex towards his desk and made him kneel down with his hands on his head.

'It's all over,' she said. 'Johanne, go back to your seat.'

'Not yet, Madame,' someone said.

It was Lolita. My heart was beating fast, fast. She stood up.

'Lolita, what are you up to? Sit down, right now!'

But Lolita pretended not to hear. She remained on her feet.

'I have something interesting to tell you,' she said.

'I'm asking you to sit down,' the teacher ordered.

But Lolita didn't budge.

'On Christmas morning there was a revolution in my house. Instead of presents under the Christmas tree, there was a suitcase next to the door. My father was in front of the television and my mother was preparing breakfast.

'"We're going on a trip?" I asked my father.

'"In a way," he said.

'"We're going to Disney World?" I asked again.

'"No, darling, that we'll do another time."

'"Oh!" I said. "So where are we going?"

'He said nothing. He got up, he hugged me very tightly, like this, then he left with his suitcase.

121

'"Daddy!" I yelled.

'But he didn't come back. Mum served me my breakfast, Kelloggs, I wasn't hungry, I was sulking. She said:

'"Lolita, you're a big girl now, and there are certain things you can understand. Your father and I, we thought it might be better to separate for a while."

'"You're getting a divorce?" I asked.

'"We're not at that point yet," she said. "But . . . "

'"Great!" I cried. "Now I'll have two homes!"'

Lolita stopped talking. Everyone was dead silent. The teacher breathed hard, rested, breathed hard, rested, then she said:

'Poor child!'

She came close to Lolita and took her in her arms.

'I'm so sorry, little one.'

'No problem, Mademoiselle. Life is full of surprises!'

Inch Allah!

◆

I went home taking Ramponeau. I stopped at number 24, since there is an empty space where tramps hole up in hordes and think they're still part of this world. They drink red wine in plastic bottles and they smoke Gitanes. They're dirtier than you and me with jackets as old as Methuselah because they're spiteful and don't want to follow the rules of society. They smell of red wine gone bad that has a particular smell. I can't stand it. The women, you'd think none of them have combed their hair since the day they were born. Me, I say they ought to shave it all. Then it can grow back afterwards. But I don't say any of that to them, seeing as no one is asking for my opinion. They drink. They laugh. They have a devil of a voice. Yes, that's it, the devil's under their skin.

An old woman passes by. She's wearing a grey coat and a black hat. When she saw the tramps, she drew back. She slung her handbag across her shoulder and held it tightly under her arm. Then she walked like an ostrich purposefully not looking in their direction. Everybody saw her. Nothing happened. The tramps burst out laughing. They had tons of crooked, blackish, and unhealthy teeth. It has always struck

122

me how white people have terrible teeth often all crooked. In my family, everybody has beautiful white teeth lined up neatly. Teeth like dogs have, well-shaped, straight, and solid. Seems that it was necessary, seeing that my ancestors were cannibals.

The business with Lolita is bugging me a lot. What with the shock of her news, and then shaking my head a little so as not to cry, and trying to understand what's happening, it all took a good bit of time, and she was already gone. Nothing can make me happier than being near her, than listening to her. That's what's in my heart. I am keeping it to myself.

◆

Lord! Since Soumana's illness, all the work falls on M'am's shoulders. She washes, she sings, she cleans, she sings, she irons, she sings, she cooks, she sings. I always wonder why tired people sing so much. M'am told me it's because they have nothing else to do.

M'am is very sweet. Never raises her voice, not one single loud word. She doesn't even complain about the work. She just works. She finds pretexts to say something nice to each kid. I swear this woman has happiness running through her body.

One day, I asked her this question:

'Why're you always happy, M'am?'

''Cause happiness, son, is like good health. It's when you don't feel anything any more.'

◆

Today, M'am is straightening out Soumana's sleeping corner. She's so weak that it's M'am who washes her, combs her hair, and treats her like a real baby. Soumana doesn't want to be touched by her. I see her eyes bulging with fury. M'am takes her clothes to the laundromat. Soumana has turned around. The old rancour makes her tremble from head to toe. She says:

'Don't touch my things! I'm not dead yet!'

'But I'm just cleaning and straightening things out a bit. . . . It's such a mess!'

'Don't touch!' she says again, her eyes shimmering. 'You'll have it all. All of it. But you could at least have the decency to wait until I've closed my eyes for good.'

'Please, Sou. Don't go through all that again.'

Bitterness gives her back her voice.

'You hate me.'

'No, Sou. I love you like you were my own daughter.'

'Yeah, sure!'

'Sou, you know I never lie. I beg you to believe that I'm not lying to you now. Allah!'

'You'll have it all ... Just be patient,' Sou says once more.

M'am is distraught. Humiliated as well. She took off her *pagnes* and I saw her belly.

'My sister' (this is the first time I hear her call her that ... There's a sob in M'am's voice. Her toothpick trembles with her chin. Her eyes are filled with tears.) 'This belly has never carried any children. For years I looked up at the sky, nothing but the sky, and I would say: "Lord!" One day, the good Lord knocked on my door. And I recognised him right away. Oh, God! It was a woman ... It was you ... In the beginning it was hard work. I was the older one, I had to put in the effort. If it was too cold to keep the window open, you'd give me a look that said: "And so what?" If the sun had set, and the light was too poor for sewing, you wouldn't budge, you'd say: "You do it." I'd comply. You took the best of everything, and you always used to serve yourself first. The best chair. The biggest piece. The prettiest tablecloth. The brightest ribbon for your hair. The loveliest dress. You'd imitate me, remember that? You used to talk and walk just like me, you'd hold your head like me. You meant more to me than my own life: you were the daughter I never had. So I'd let it go ... Take it, take it, M'am doesn't need anything. Then you touched something else, something terrible, you touched my man ... Yes, the man of my life. The first time he left me for your bed, I was too taken aback to feel any hurt. Then you wanted him, you wanted him more and more, and he let it happen. I couldn't bear it any more ... I had nothing left to give. And that's when I hated you. Not for very long, of course! You had children – my children – and I couldn't. Nobody can hate the good Lord! I'm a mother and it's thanks to you. I will never be able to thank you enough for that.'

Soumana looked at her. There was a curious glint in her eyes. She burst out laughing.

I met Star during the first weeks after my arrival in your country. I had come alone. I had left my own people behind and was skimming your soil with a few photographs and smells as my only reminder. The scent of ripe mangoes. Of avocados. Of custard-apples. The smell of rain mingled with soil, nubile and tender. They would tell the suspended story. Uprooting is hard.

They would accompany me everywhere. They used to give me the feeling that I did exist a little. Living the dream burrowed deep inside the sky. The split is hard. The break. The wound.

In the streets, passers-by, cars. I would stagger. I would hold on to the walls, themselves unsteady. All I used to know about cities was what I'd heard. All I knew about the sky was the azure blue and the sun which beat down. And about women, pagnes in colours of the gardens, all I knew was laughter, that ephemeral veil drifting up to the sky.

I used to see the women, your women. They would look at me, their eyes vague as if stupefied by some unknown tranquilliser. I didn't yet know then that I was transparent. I would see their long hair falling down freely, I'd hear the wind carrying it along. I had no horizon.

You'll tell me they could break through my loneliness.

Always exoticism. Sometimes a lay. Tenderness, never!

My chest was growing colder, forming a block of ice that was covering the treasure hidden there, where the heart lies.

There was the one from Pigalle with her plastic hose. They said she had something special in her look and her fingers. She had the gift of reviving a dead sex organ.

She was small, with breasts like two lemons and buttocks as plump as the bottom of a cooking pot.

She would serve me stew in peanut sauce.

126

She would kiss my parched lips. She would spread her legs and look away. Ungraciously she'd play the whore for this nigger.

And then Star came. She came out of my imagination so that the dream would survive.

One had to continue to believe in the beauties of these places, deprived of life, feeble in their generosity.

And so Star came. A small brunette with sunshine hair in the black forest of time. We were inside, under the canopy. The noises from outside weren't reaching us. Isolated. Protected. She wouldn't speak. Out of decency and because of a proper education. Submissive. Never triumphant. Nor rebellious. And out of this prison of ecstasy sprang as many brooks as there were nights we'd spend together and this would irrigate my days without poetry.

Then M'am arrived. The image disappeared. Today I need her to survive. But she flees from me.

(Abdou Traoré)

This evening, the whole black tribe has come. A kind of high tide of people, about fifty of them. They're daubed with colour. Some are wearing mud. They've brought palm wine, cola nuts, red hens, mangoes, and avocados. They put Soumana on a mat. We all sat down, women and children in the back, the men up front. There was a whispered discussion between Cérif, the king of the marabouts, and my dad. Dinner was around eight o'clock, stew in peanut sauce and rice which we ate with our fingers. The most important part of this ceremony was devoted to the cola nut. The cola is the symbol of harmony, peace, and happiness among my people. In olden days, it was upon this nut that our empires were constructed. It bodes well. Everything began a very, very long time ago. In my village, people used to live in harmony out of respect for the gods. They used to cultivate millet, manioc, peanuts, all of which grows well, and many other things, too. And everybody shared everything, according to their needs. One day, a chief from a neighbouring village wanted more than his own harvest. He wanted more lands so that he could barter with the white people who were settling on the coast. He annexed more and more lands. He increased the number of his wives so that they could work for him. But soon the other villagers had nothing left to eat any more, because the chief had taken all their arable and fertile land. One morning, they called the family council together. They decided they had to get rid of the go-getter. But he was not alone. He had all the white people with him and they had rifles. So the war began. Large numbers of Malinke died in it. Famine was threatening.

There was nothing left to eat in the granaries. Some fled from the villages. Others were eaten by wild animals as they ran off. The people were threatened with extinction. The ambitious chief continued to cultivate his lands. He grew richer. One day, the village madwoman went to throw a cola nut in front of the go-getter's door. His oldest son died. And every day, she returned to throw one nut and each time someone in the chief's family would die. Soon, all his children, all his wives died without knowing how or why. Then his own health began to fail. He had nothing left, no money, no honour. He called for the Malinke chief and he gathered all the villagers around him.

'Do you want to live in happiness, health, contentment, joy, without the ills of which you complain, rich in abundance and without unhappiness? Follow this principle. Confess as if you were at the hour of your death, observe the definition of justice and give to everyone what is his; live by the sweat of your brow and not of the brow of another; help yourself to what you yourself have properly earned in payment and goods. Then you shall live in joy, you shall be happy, and everything will thrive in your hands. I have erred, my brothers. Your tears, your sorrows did not open my eyes. Only the nut reminded me that I had cracked the core of an indivisible whole. Farewell, my brothers, and may this nut be forevermore the symbol of peace, obedience, and harmony for us.'

Thereupon he died. No one mourned him. He was buried without dignity. And my village then found its prosperity again.

It was the marabout Cérif who told us this story before he began his treatment. He made Soumana drink some potion, then he dipped his fingers in the bowl, he took a few drops of the concoction, sprinkled it on Soumana to give her his blessing. Then the party began. Not a real party, of course, but that's an expression that means they began to dance around her making a lot of noise with a drum. It was a very lovely feast. Such as I've never seen in Belleville before. Soumana was watching it all in dismay. As if she were already no longer there, as if she were alone somewhere else. The black folks were happy and yelling as best they could. Monsieur Cérif says that the noise was scaring away the demon who has come to steal Soumana's soul. With the palm wine, the dancing lasted all night long.

Black people love palm wine. All over Africa. If you don't succeed in making them do what you want when you've tried everything else, just mention palm wine, a small calabash-full for example. Or if you want to get them to do something really important, chat with them about palm wine.

Monsieur Cérif offered up prayers to our gods, impatiently awaiting a change in the situation. But Soumana was good for nothing any more and we just had to let her be. Monsieur Cérif says that the attempt had failed because Soumana had offended God, which made her soul unclean so it couldn't be healed. And that's how we stayed up until morning, facing the Malinke gods. The tribe was disappointed. With one and the same gesture they wiped the smiles off their faces and the sweat from their brows and went home with words of encouragement for us.

I was so exhausted, falling over from sleepiness, my belly filled with chicken in peanut sauce and palm wine, and my ears so full of all that singing that I don't even know which way to turn any more.

I really wonder what you're going to think of all this.

On this earth where I shall be a stranger forever, I have tried to be a good Muslim husband. I have balanced my preferences. I have two wives but I've done everything I could to make one as much of a favourite as the other. I have divided my earnings equitably between them. I was careful in handling the delicate task of the double agent: the secretive ways in which I would go to kiss one for fear that the other one would find out and could – justifiably so – have given me a hard time.

Veiled, protected from the outside world, withdrawn and on their knees, I freed them from the evil of men. Minor unkindnesses, exclusion, even self-centredness were of no concern to them any longer. A kind of immunity. Which sheltered them from the judgement of men.

One day, I wanted to check this immune state. I took them to a nightclub run by a compatriot, a black man from our country. It was their first time. They knew nothing about dissolute places like this. Nor about the barely noticeable cracks between the walls. Nor the thousands of tricks of these bare-legged women, with their red-painted nails, easy beauties whom I suspect of putting on their passions along with their necklaces and purses. No one seemed to have noticed that the women who loved me were there. And yet they were there, concealed behind the curtains of their immunity, they were spying upon the hubbub of this unknown world with curiosity, the sound of voices, the talk, the burst of anger or a laugh, and the kisses in half-dark places.

They didn't dance. They chatted in a stage whisper and very quickly they said it was hot. And we left the club.

On the way home they were satisfied. And like shadows, they imitated the dance steps, the excessive hip-swaying of the whore-

women, the feigned anger and the disguised pleasures, and they
thanked heaven they had been spared all this. What else could I do,
friend?

I have been a good Muslim husband.

(Abdou Traoré)

Mademoiselle Garnier came back. Lord, how skinny she is! You'd
think she was a piece of board. School has picked up again. Except
that Lolita is pretty sad. She's becoming a bad student and during
break she talks to nobody. She stays all by herself in a corner. It seems
that everything throws her off-track and worries her. I'm trying to give
her some attention but I don't much dare.

Aminata (I still can't manage to call her mum) came to fetch us so
we can hear her, dad and I. She took us to a kind of club where she is
singing. First some songs by Mireille Mathieu. Then some she's made
up herself. She has the kind of voice you'd never think could sing.
Thin and high-pitched, she sounds like a wounded bird. But it doesn't
bother Aminata. Nor the men who are there. And I got used to it later.
In the end I even liked it. Really not bad at all. Dad was dumbfounded.
He couldn't get over it.

'It's an odd sensation,' he told me. 'Just like that, all of a sudden,
she starts to sing without any warning.'

'You didn't really expect her to send you a registered letter about it,
did you?' I answered.

'True, son. But really! It's so weird. It makes me think of a parrot.
There he is in his cage for years on end, says nothing. And then one
morning, just when you don't want people to know your name is
Thingamajig, he starts to sing your name and the police nab you.'

'Say, dad, do you think she's angry with Soumana for having thrown
her out?'

'I'm sure she is. But what's it matter? Aminata isn't bad, and she
knows perfectly well life isn't always fun.'

'Yeah,' I went. 'I like her a lot, Aminata.'

'Hmmmmm,' he said, seeming surprised. 'I really wonder why she
came back, that one.'

'Because she loves me.'

'That must be it . . .'

At that point, Aminata started to sing:

I am whore, that's my name
I am whore, that's my name
as if whore were a name
if whore is a name,
then jerk is the name of a guy
and if I call him you poor jerk
he's sure to beat me up . . .

◆

Today after break, Lolita didn't come back to class.

It's raining.

She stayed in the courtyard near the tall pole and she's crying.

It's still raining.

I don't know what on earth to do. I go out, put my hands on her shoulders, I say:

'Don't cry.'

She pulls away. She runs off. I run after her. It's cold as hell. It takes me a long time to figure out I'm not wearing anything. The courtyard is empty.

It's still raining.

I see the rain droplets crashing on Lolita's head. She runs all the way to the gym. All the lights are off. It takes me some time to get used to the darkness. She sits down on the cement. She looks at me, but it's as if she doesn't see me. She says nothing.

'Do you have a dog only you can see?' I ask.

She says nothing.

'Me, I have a dog. His name is Superman. When I'm upset, I call him, then he jumps on me, he gives me lots of kisses and then I'm not sad any more. I can call him and he'll give you kisses and then you won't be upset any more. Not at all. No more.'

Still, she says nothing.

So I sit down next to her. I take her hand. I'm waiting for her to come back. And I say:

'Lolita!'

There, she's coming back. She tilts her head like this on my shoulder. She is crying. I'm overcome, she's crying and I'm overcome. I get closer to her. I turn her face towards me like that and I say:

'Look at me!' as if in authority, but the other side of authority is tenderness.

She lowers her eyes.

'What do you want?' I ask. 'Why are you crying?'

'Why? Why?' she asks.

Then she yells:

'Why do adults have to hurt children?'

'Because they're parents,' I say. 'That gives them every right.'

'I don't want parents any more,' she says. 'I don't want them any more.'

Outside it is still raining.

I'm struck with helpless stupor . . . Angry, too, because I don't know what to say to console her.

I put my hands on her shoulders, and since she says nothing I put my hand on her hair.

Outside, it is still raining.

I hold her close to my chest, hug her tightly, I can hardly breathe any more so big is my heart inside my chest, and I say: 'Don't be afraid, my Lolita. As long as I'm here, no harm will come to you. I have fetishes, you know. D'you want one of them?'

She looks at me with her large eyes. And it was heaven itself looking at me, with its moon, its stars, its galaxies, and everything else. I lay my head on her shoulder. And I rest my head on her shoulder. I pull her towards me, close to me. My heart turns over. She pulls at my shirt. It's sweet, so supersweet. I felt I was flying, flying like a bird, maybe that's what happiness is?

'I love you,' Lolita says.

'Don't be sad any more,' I answer.

'I'm not sad any more. Not any more. Not at all.'

She smacks her mouth against my mouth. Her hands are feeling my trousers, like that, like that, it feels good, and I get goose pimples.

133

'Shocking! Shocking!'

Someone is shrieking behind my back.

I turn around. It's the snooper. She is the cleaning woman at school and she gossips for two, so everybody despises her. Always something to tell the principal to get on the right side of him.

She lunges towards me and pushes me. I fall flat on my nose on the cement. She snatches at Lolita:

'Aren't you ashamed of yourself?' she says to her. 'At your age doing . . .'

'Leave her alone!' I say.

'Shut up, you dirty nigger,' she screams.

I kick her hard in the legs. But she throws me on the ground and I cannot defend myself any longer.

'How outrageous!' she shrieks. 'Outrageous! Outrageous!'

Then she leaves, still shrieking.

Lolita is on her knees, her face against the floor like a dancer at the Opera. She's crying. She's crying and you'd think there's nothing else she's capable of doing. And I, I imagine her dancing on the moon in a lovely white dress.

'Don't you love me any more?' I ask.

'That's not it,' she says. 'After you, only Danone can do that to me.'

'So why're you crying?'

She doesn't answer.

Outside, it's still raining.

'It's because you don't love me any more.'

She looks at me with tear-filled eyes and she says to me:

'Oh, Mamadou, what's going to become of us?'

'Don't worry. I'll take care of everything.'

◆

My dad was summoned by the principal of my school. He's angry and hits the wall from time to time with his fists. Sure he's dying to let someone have it. My sisters are staying very quiet. M'am is too old. Soumana is sicker and sicker, so . . . And Mademoiselle Esther who is here since yesterday is not in good shape. Her belly is growing rounder all the time.

'When are you due?' they ask her.

'In three months,' she answers. And takes another grape.

I know, *Allah*! that Mademoiselle Garnier betrayed my confidence again. But I don't want to get into confessions.

Father is dressed up to the nines. You've got to understand. The principal isn't just anybody.

In front of the office, there's Lolita's mother too, except that she's wearing jeans and basketball shoes. She's sitting down. She's seen me at her house. When she thinks I'm not watching her, she throws me odd looks like I was a curious animal. My dad goes to the main door, comes back again, fiddles with his hat, looks at his watch. Right at the moment that I least expect it, Lolita's mum asks him:

'Are you Monsieur Abdou?'

'Yes, Madame,' he answers.

'I am Lolita's mother, she is in your son's class.'

They exchange a lengthy smile. I know it's not a real smile. It's not the time for pleasantries. After that, they've got nothing else to say to each other.

That's when the principal comes out of his office and says:

'Come in . . . come in, and please sit down.'

Our parents go in. Lolita and I stay outside. At first she doesn't look at me. It's as if there is a kind of sheet between us. An old bedspread or something else I haven't seen. My first thought was: I'm going to pull it away. I'm going to see her beautiful eyes. But I didn't have the time. I'd just moved one arm forward when she raised her head, looked at me and looked at me, then said:

'Mamadou, my mum is making me change schools.'

I pull my arm back. It falls down beside my body. In any case, there's nothing left to pull away. I don't know what to do any more. I'm plonked there in the middle of the hallway with lots of things going around in my head. Who would have believed that! I say to myself.

'It's because of what happened. Mademoiselle was at the house yesterday. She told her everything.'

I had tears in my eyes. Lolita looks at me with her skyblue eyes. She raises her hands and wipes my tears and says:

'Did your mother make onion soup last night?'

135

'Yeah, I think so. She probably did make onion soup last night.'

That's all I was able to say. Then she went like this, here on my head, and pulled me close to her. She smells like M'am.

Someone said:

'Oh, no! You're not starting that again!'

It is Lolita's mum. In her eyes I can see that I'm guilty. That it is all my fault. That it's because of me that I love Lolita and Lolita loves me. I'm guilty of loving. That says it all.

My dad shouts:

'I'm going to teach you how to live, you . . . You . . .'

He has no more words. Words like hammers would be needed to make me understand, but he doesn't have any. He lurches towards me.

'Take it easy, sir!' the principal yells.

'Take it easy!' goes Lolita's mum, that hypocrite.

Finally he calms down. But only like a snake that waits until your feet come close enough for him to bite you. I'm not taking any chances. I move away. They began to talk. Everyone is of the opinion that it's all because of moral depravity, because of television and all the bad things we see. They called it negative influences or something like that, which I didn't really understand. They spent a good bit longer searching for reasons. In the end, they came to the conclusion that kids are a real problem, ungrateful, and all that . . .

If you can explain all this to me, you will have my eternal gratitude.

I am lost, friend. What is to be done? I stand perplexed before your traditions which I neither want to offend nor understand, for fear of both getting lost in them and ruining my faith, the strongest I have, strong beyond compare. It is all that I have left, my friend. That I used to have left. And even there, in that faith of mine, in spite of myself, in spite of everything, time has been conjugated into the past and into the future like the tense of a verb.

I bear you no grudges, friend. Besides, I love you with exquisite indulgence. Your vocabulary, your mores, your haste, the crazy timetable of your beliefs offend my feelings. I keep quiet. Above all, I didn't want you to come and track me down where I am and prevent me from being holy when I can. But you are waging war upon me. Your perfected machinery is invading my house. Your ideas. Your beliefs. Your habits. Today my body is tattooed with so many questions. Snatches of insanity hang on to my lips.

My wives are sulking and turning the geography of my home upside down. Misfortune! However it never rains but it pours. There is my son inventing other languages for me. He is forcing a shift in the relationships. He is turning relationships over to my disadvantage. He is weaving networks of priorities, his secret codes of reference and contempt.

The thing happened without my knowing it, too. It infiltrated my life, insidious, surreptitious, as imperceptible as the oozing through an old roof.

You know, friend, a ridiculed father is like a jealous husband. I learn about my misfortune from new indecencies, from the clashing choice of vocabulary, from games, from barely perceptible signs. My son has rounded a headland. In the wrong direction.

He is reluctant to put on his djellaba. He wants clothes like those of

Stallone, exactly the same, for fear that he'll feel lost. His dancing, the crudeness of which astounds me, is just like the contortions of the stars on television, and that's not all!

I have been invaded, friend, I am losing myself.

(Abdou Traoré)

Spring is here. It's beautiful. A bit cool as always towards Easter. Everything is already quite green in Paris. It's pretty. And towards evening, all the immigrants go out on the boulevard de Belleville. Some settle down in the cafés. They talk. They stay silent. They have nothing to say to each other. Except about everyday life. They watch the girls go by. A few of them say vulgar things about the low-slung behind of some woman or the way another walks. Immigrants are very keen on that. They talk about it all the time. You got to understand. It's easier for them to talk than to act, seeing that most of them have left their wives in Africa.

Me, I'm at my worst: Lolita no longer looks at me. She talks to nobody. At break I wink at her. But you'd think that her eyes have been remote-controlled not to see me. I'm tormented. By love. And by the lack of it. Maybe she never did love me? Sometimes I think Lolita never loved me, and I really wonder what there is to love anyway. My hair is frizzy. My skin is very dark. My nose is nothing special. Same goes for my lips. My body is the body of a little boy. No great muscles. No blond curls. But my heart has to be very large, for enclosed within it lie flowers of blood.

I talk to myself quite often. I tell myself that she's the first white girl I've ever known and that all of it is very new to me. What do you want? My dad says you can get used to anything, to hunger, to thirst, to smells, to everything really! It couldn't all have just gone like clockwork right away! We should realise that.

Not so much as a look. Not a word. Nothing is organised for people to meet one another, Monsieur Ndongala always says. Wars everywhere, and assassinations. Yet, sometimes I dream. I dream that Lolita loves me, she loves me too. That she hasn't forgotten a thing. So then I write to her in my head. I start my letter: 'Dear Lolita', right in the

138

middle of the courtyard or while I watch television, or at night as I'm falling asleep. 'Dear, very dear Lolita', and I imagine she's receiving my letters and that she answers me: 'Dear Mamadou, this is what's going on in my head . . .'

After the scandal, I didn't dare do anything more. I'm just waiting for my fate, seeing that it's none of my business.

◆

When school finished, I went to Monsieur Guillaume's café. Madame Saddock is there and I act as if I hadn't seen her. After all, is she finally going to let go of us? Monsieur Ndongala is there as well. He's super elegant. He's wearing black trousers with red braces and a bow tie. He's with my uncle. They're conversing. Conversing is perhaps not the right word. I can't tell whether uncle is shouting or preaching seeing him wave his arms around like that. At the end of it all, he moves his hand over his face, impatient, as if he's wiping the sweat off. His face is shaded. Probably, if he had a woman near him, he'd have smacked her one.

'D'you realise?' Uncle Kouam says. 'She's cheating on me with a woman!'

'That doesn't count,' goes Doctor Ndongala. 'With women it's all a question of circumstances. It's enough for a man just to be there at the right moment and . . .'

I pull up a chair.

'You really think so? Maybe, maybe that's so. I must say, as far as getting laid goes, she had nothing to complain about.'

'You know, friend, with women, you shouldn't go overboard. My word! . . .'

I sit down.

'I'm telling you, she got plenty. Listen, just barely two months ago I ordered "Skin force 3". And with that, pal, she can really feel you!'

'What's that?' Doctor Ndongala asks.

'Man, I tell you, it's a medicine I saw advertised in some magazine, I don't remember where. "Get back the strength and power you had at twenty!" it said, and it showed a nice-looking girl with tits like you wouldn't believe and then it explained you could have it all back and

139

begin to chase skirts again even if you'd found yourself a bit shaky before. So, I told myself I wouldn't mind trying a little of that. I can't begin to tell you about the result, my boy! In comparison, a horse would be a joke! You'd better try some of it yourself. But, of course, it's not my place to give advice to a doctor.'

Looking as if he were thinking of something else, Doctor Ndongala fiddles with his bow tie, as if he wanted to be sure it was still in place. He doesn't take his eyes off him. And my uncle Kouam says:

'So, old man, you're sure you really don't want to give it a try?'

Monsieur Ndongala fiddles with his moustache. Then he goes:

'I'm not better hung than anyone else. But while we're on the subject, I can assure you I don't need any medication or anything else. I've always had more than one woman, that's not to say I don't love 'em. I do love 'em, each one in her own way. And I thank God that he has made me understand that love is not a question of tits and arses. It surprises me you still love Mathilda after all the tricks she's pulled on you! Did she bewitch you or what?'

'Bewitch, no. But I do have regrets.'

'Oh yes?'

'Yeah. I've put her through some pretty outrageous things, you know.'

'Like what?'

'I cheated on her.'

'Everybody does that,' says Monsieur Ndongala. 'That's not a crime!'

'In this particular case it is, since her parents never wanted to see her again after our marriage.'

'Well, all you have to do is go and apologise to her, buy her flowers . . .'

'No flowers,' Monsieur Guillaume cuts in. 'When you give flowers to a woman, she immediately thinks that you have something you want to be forgiven for; believe me, I have a lot of experience with that.'

'In any case she doesn't want to see me any more,' says my uncle Kouam. 'It won't do any good!'

'I bet she still has feelings for you.'

'Pfff!'

'Yes, yes,' Monsieur Ndongala insists. 'Women are as phoney as photocopies, word of honour.'

'She's threatened to kill me if I come within ten paces of her.'

'Crap!' Monsieur Ndongala exclaims.

'Me, if I were in your place, I wouldn't think it was crap,' says Monsieur Guillaume. 'You should read the papers, you'll understand.'

'Oh yes?' asks my uncle Kouam.

Monsieur Guillaume sighs, then says:

'Just today I read this in the paper: "A man was found dead in the forest of Fontainebleau. It is not known who killed him." I bet it was his ex whom he must have given a hard time.'

My uncle frowns, then he says:

'I'm an idiot. If I could do it all over again . . . Well, after all, I didn't know before . . . Now I know that . . .'

'You need experience in everything, my friend,' says Monsieur Guillaume. 'You're lucky that at least you learn your lesson from your mistakes.'

'I'm really sorry that she left you,' says Monsieur Ndongala. 'I know what it's like. Oh, yes, I know all about that department too.'

'How's it going, Loukoum?' Monsieur Ndongala asks as he suddenly turns round to me.

'Very well, thank you,' I answer like a good citizen.

'And school, things all right?' asks my uncle Kouam.

'All right,' I answer.

'You been here long?'

'No, uncle,' I say.

'So much the better!' he goes as he exchanges an odd look with Monsieur Ndongala.

Adults are definitely strange!

◆

At home everything is going badly. Soumana is sick, sicker than a dog, and M'am is like an overburdened donkey, since everything falls on her shoulders, the children, the housework, and all the rest of it. She's becoming a true Parisian because she no longer has time, not for singing, not for anything, and all she does is run after one thing or another. My dad acts as if he doesn't see it. He continues to go out, looking as if nothing's wrong. Sometimes I do help M'am. But certain things I shouldn't do because I am a man.

My uncle Kouam no longer leaves our house. It's as if he were glued to his chair ever since my aunt Mathilda split. In the beginning he wept. Then he didn't talk about it any more. He's just sad but we're used to that in this family and it's nothing new. He goes to the office at seven in the morning and comes home late at night. Even Monsieur Guillaume's café doesn't interest him any more. Sometimes he stays in his corner and talks to himself.

'What're you doing?' M'am asks him one day.

'I'm cooking up something,' he answers.

But he doesn't tell us what.

Two weeks later, there he is with a yardstick measuring the entire house.

'Are you finally going to tell me what you're up to?' M'am asks him.

'I'm setting up a bio-chemical plant.'

'Here in Belleville?' M'am asks in astonishment.

'In this dump?' he answers with a snigger. 'Rest assured, I'm going to set it up in Conakry. It'll run like a dream!'

'If there's a greater dump than Conakry, I'll die,' says M'am.

Me, I haven't a clue where Conakry is, so I keep my mouth shut. Besides, nobody is asking for my opinion.

'Africa is booming,' says my uncle. 'And Conakry is the capital of Africa.'

'Have you asked your wife's opinion? She's white, it may well be she doesn't want to live in the heat and humidity and with the mosquitoes we have there.'

'I no longer have a wife,' my uncle said.

He began to measure our place again and his eyes betrayed confusion.

I don't know anything, friend. Not even that the earth is round. That the sun doesn't move even though it seems to rise and set. I don't know about these three people in one. I don't know what electric current is. Nor why stones fall back to the ground. I don't know how to read French. I don't know why night replaces day nor why I prefer yams to Brussels sprouts. I know nothing. But I can repeat this to you persistently: 'That my son is my blood. I have seen his life, this life which I have passed on to him, I know that he is the most precious of my earthly possessions, the only one I possess in my own right. He was still nothing but an apple, a mouse, a frog when I was working on finding myself back in him. Is that not every father's right? My son. My continuity. I had to make him become an imitation of me. For better or for worse, his character had to flow out of mine, as in a palm plantation where the geometry is created by unharvested trees and fascinating shapes.'

Is it too much to ask that a son be the image of the father?

When he was very young, I would take my son with me to teach him the secrets of our gods, as if in a forest, walking lithely without paying attention to the brick buildings, the car horns, the shop windows, the noisy crowd. I would teach him to distinguish other things, more essential things in my eyes: the weather, storms, the colour of a pale sun. He used to trust me. He would hold my hand, trotting straight along.

I would say to him:

At home, in Mali, the streets are narrower, bordered with mango and avocado trees.

At mealtimes, the compounds, like chimneys, exhale their pungent perfumes of hot pepper and spices.

143

There's a big square with a baobab tree a thousand years old that watches over the tribe.

Under the verandahs at siesta time, crouched on their mats smelling of hay, the old men murmur their prayers.

But you know, friend, little by little my son was no longer listening to me. Or when he lent me an ear it was with a pout, the pout of a television announcer.

I've known the tragedies of my religion for too long, I've struggled alone for too long against Christianity.

Today I see my son.

He has discovered the vocabulary of Paris. Words scratched in by wind and weather.

He has acquired other ways of saying hello.

He knows rituals that throw me.

He feels repugnance at eating with his hands.

He imposes other conformities.

He imports tastes, preoccupations.

He passes from one universe to the other without worrying about it. He judges ours, feels contempt. My stories amuse him. Africa, Mali, my Land. Our Land – God's creation – all these things belong only to God – those splendours which night completes, the quiet moment in which the buried, naked dead come back to earth.

We have come from the Nile, my son.

The Pharaohs had made us into slaves.

Islam liberated us.

From then on, we have belonged to the Malinke tribe.

Friend, my son no longer listens to me. I feel emptied of myself, robbed and ransacked of my last dream, to the last of what is beautiful.

No, friend, I have no taste for worlds that reel with uncertainties.

I don't know how to withstand so much outside interference.

I don't know how to withstand so many subversions.

I don't know how to renegotiate the constraints and adjust myself to them.

I believe I'm going mad.

(Abdou Traoré)

I'm on holiday. M'am cooks. My dad is with Monsieur Cérif. There they are looking at each other, chewing cola without talking. Aminata is there too. She is humming something while doing her nails. She has made up her lips so red you wouldn't believe it, and her hair's all tousled like someone who's just woken up. She's not got anything on other than some sort of rompers which are nothing more than small shorts held up by braces that go around her chest. The shorts cover hardly any of her long legs. She makes you think a little of a very ripe mango, when you see how well she fills her little shorts and the thing she's wearing over her chest, and how all of it is smooth chestnut-coloured and plump.

She looks up and says to me:

'Come into my arms, my baby . . . I want you . . .' she says.

Me, I don't budge. She comes and takes me in her arms. She touches my hair. She takes me on her knees, which feels really weird because after all, I'm ten years old . . . So I excuse myself. She insists. The doorbell rings. I go to open the door. It's my uncle Kouam. He looks at Aminata and I hear him saying under his breath: 'Oh, for heaven's sake!' as if he were talking to himself. Right then his eyes meet my father's which are so calm you'd think they were dead. And he says:

'Such misfortune!'

'Shouldn't say misfortune,' Aminata says. 'It's asleep, don't wake it up.'

Everyone looked at her as if she were a ghost and her voice were coming from the tomb.

Nobody really grasps her too well. First of all, she says everything that comes into her head, even if it isn't polite. Sometimes my dad looks at her when he knows nobody sees him.

Today he says:

'There's some conduct I do not tolerate under my roof.'

And off he goes: 'My wife shall not do this, my wife must not do that . . . I never let my wife do this . . .'

Aminata snorts, then she says with a big smile:

'Well then, lucky for you I'm not your wife.'

Everyone looks at her again, you'd think she was threatening the world with lightning, floods, and earthquakes.

'Excuse me,' she says, still sniggering with laughter.

Then she puts her hand over her mouth. She lowers her head.

M'am has prepared fish with rice. Everyone sat down on the floor just like at a picnic. And we feasted with our hands because without a fork you can smell the aroma better. The women sat down with us. It's because of the misfortune. Things are upside-down and no one knows who is who any longer.

Monsieur Cérif bent his head and began to recite a prayer. While he was talking, Aminata stretched out her arm and grabbed a big fish head, then she started to eat. Really, she has no manners and everyone looked at her, and then looked away and pretended she wasn't there. Yes, she was sitting down as well, eating noisily, but it was as if she weren't there, she really had no place here seeing that she had no manners. My sisters were passing food to each other, their arms going back and forth right under her nose, as if she weren't there. They call M'am 'Mummy', but they call Aminata 'Madame'. The only one who pays any attention to her at all is uncle Kouam. He is sitting facing her and looks at her secretly.

At the end of the meal, Aminata gets up. She lights a cigarette. She takes one drag, then says:

'Well, it's time I brought you up to date now.'

'About what?' asks uncle Kouam.

'I'm going away and Loukoum is coming with me.'

My dad turns his head towards her in one motion.

'What're you talking about?' he asks.

'Loukoum is coming to live with me for a few days, I said. I've a friend who's letting me use his house in the country. Not far from Paris. It's green there and there are animals. Nothing better for a kid.'

'Over my dead body.'

'As you wish,' says Aminata without getting upset. 'But it's really stupid of you. All our great men, Mitterrand, de Gaulle, Senghor, Delon, Frank Sinatra, Martin Luther King, all of them grew up on a farm. Think about it, it's ideal for a kid: feeding the chickens, geese, ducks, milking the cows, horse-riding . . .'

Then Aminata stops, her words catch in her throat a bit and she says:

'Come to think of it, there aren't any horses. My friend Malim Hassey can't stand them, not even in a picture. Donkeys galore,

146

though. I ask you, Abdou, can you picture a healthier, more invigorating environment for a growing boy?'

Aminata has tears in her eyes just from imagining how invigorating it's going to be down there.

Father looks at me, acts as if he's about to get up, then looks at the tart, then looks at M'am.

'It's your son, after all,' he says to M'am.

'Yeah,' she answers. 'But I believe a child needs his mother, his real mother I mean. And as for your dead body, I actually need a doormat by the front door.'

'What? What's that you're saying?'

The others remain seated around the picnic, their mouths wide open.

'That you're self-centred, a washout, and that it's high time you paid attention to what's happening around you, that's what I'm saying.'

Father splutters.

'But . . .'

'No buts. Aminata can take the kid for a few days. Of course I'm going to miss him, but I've had my share of misery in this world, enough to keep me laughing for the rest of my days.'

'Take him away then! You're talking rubbish.'

'Hey there, just a minute!' goes uncle Kouam.

'You, shut up! If you hadn't been so eager to boss your wife around, she wouldn't have left you for a woman.'

'That's not a true wife. A woman who doesn't give a shit about what other people might think . . .'

"She's her own boss, that's all,' M'am says.

Then he lowers his head.

Me, I've stopped chewing I'm so overcome by M'am's tone.

'Oh, no. No! This is too much! Either she goes or I go,' Monsieur Cérif says as he bangs his two fists on the mat.

Under the circumstances, that really worries me, for there'll be no one left to chase away the demons from Soumana. Then I ask my uncle Kouam in a whisper, so Monsieur Cérif won't hear me:

'You really think he's going to leave?'

'No way! From what I can see, you didn't get it at all, my boy. He's

147

the kind of guy who's got it into his head that it's his duty to track down sin all over the place and then afterwards to stay glued to the place and watch over it constantly, so he can always put the blame on it for something and can never think of anything else.'

'You're right,' I say.

'Don't worry about Cérif. He likes money too much, and it's not by waggling a black bottom under his nose and by talking obscenities that the devil will manage to chase him away from here.'

They discussed things a while longer and finally agreed with Aminata on the stay at the farm and allowed me to go. But father warned her that if she didn't behave properly or was going to attract the least little problem she wasn't ever going to see me again. M'am packed for me. Uncle Kouam suggested he drop us off, so he took my bag. My dad looked at him in a really strange way and said he'd walk us to the car.

Aminata is walking ahead. It's funny how her arse is bouncing around inside her rompers. We went downstairs in silence, except for uncle Kouam who'd say from time to time: 'For heaven's sake!' As if to himself. Under his breath.

And while we're going down the staircase, I ask my dad:

'She really is nice, my mum. D'you think she earns a lot of money?'

'In her profession, I'd be surprised if she didn't have any,' he answers. 'But it's dangerous,' he adds, giving uncle Kouam a long hard look.

'Is it catching?' I ask.

'Not the profession, son, but the diseases are.' (With those words he stops and calmly looks uncle Kouam over.) 'And I think you've got enough good sense not to get involved with such foolishness.'

Whereupon he smacks a kiss on my forehead and goes back up to the house.

I raise my head and see Madame Saddock who pretends to be counting the cars on the pavement across the street. She doesn't give up, that one! It's true, though, white people never admit they've been defeated, that's what my dad said. What a pain!

We got into the car and all of a sudden Madame Saddock comes running over to us.

'Loukoum! Loukoum!' she yells.

'Who's she?' Aminata asks. 'You know her?'

'Yeah . . . Pff,' I go.

Madame Saddock leans her fat head towards the window and asks:

'You're going on a trip?'

'Well yes, Madame.'

'I'm taking my son on holiday,' Aminata goes. 'We're going to the country. Nothing more invigorating for a kid. I'm sure he'll come back bursting with energy.'

'Your son?' Madame Saddock asks, her face showing she can't get over it.

'Well, yes Madame,' Aminata says bursting with laughter. 'What's so strange about that?'

Madame Saddock muttered something under her breath but nobody heard it since my uncle drove off at that very moment.

We left but got lost in the traffic and then didn't know where we were any more. Paris is a lot bigger than any other place. And there are so many streets and cars that when you begin to drive round it all, you could certainly sleep there and starve, too, without anyone taking notice. It didn't take long for us to be stuck in a street with lots of stores full of elegant clothes. My uncle Kouam yelled to call a cop in a navy blue uniform who was holding his cap underneath his arm.

'What's the name of this street?' my uncle asks.

'The Faubourg-Saint-Honoré, Sir,' he answers, with a haughty look.

'Well, how do we get to Montaban-les-Oies?'

'Pfff,' the cop says. 'That's complicated. Wait a minute.'

'That's the trouble with these godforsaken dumps,' my uncle Kouam says. 'Wherever you want to go, you're stuck before you even get there. It would be best to go there tomorrow, it'll be easier.'

'Absolutely,' Aminata says, almost jumping with joy. 'Take us home.'

'Home?' I ask. 'We're not going to your friend Malim Hassey's farm any more?'

'You crazy? I only said that to intimidate that idiot Abdou.'

Still, I was sad, seeing that the thought of living on a farm had made me quite happy. But I said nothing. It doesn't pay to discuss things with a woman when she's made up her mind. Finally, we took Montparnasse. My uncle Kouam was preoccupied. Something was bothering him. You could tell. But it was really funny, since he wouldn't stop saying: 'For heaven's sake!' And mumbling God only knows what else. At one point we almost ran into a six-ton truck. My uncle Kouam jams on the brakes. The truck driver puffs up his cheeks and becomes all red in the face.

'Son-of-a-bitch!' he screams. 'You're not in Ouagadougou here!'

'Nobody gives a damn!' uncle shouts back.

'What was that?' the driver asks.

'You're an arsehole!'

The truck driver moves his truck a little. Behind us, people are honking their horns and treating uncle Kouam like a pigheaded so and so. The truck driver comes running at us trying to dodge all the cars, his face even redder than before. In front of us the street has emptied out a bit. Uncle Kouam waits till he gets close. Then he raises a finger and goes: 'Tssss!', then takes off like a rocket and gets through the junction just before the light turns red. After that we make a turn and as for the truck driver, we never saw him again.

Aminata is in heaven. She laughs, turns around and kisses my face three or four times. She lowers the window. She sticks her head out and smiles broadly at everybody on the pavement.

'These white folks are killing! They've got the gall to make us think that it's our fault if Africa is poor. As if we're not smart enough to get by. As if all we do is sleep, get laid, and never do any work. I'd really like to know why they needed black slaves to get by in the Americas, if they work so hard themselves.'

'Mmmmmm . . . Mmmmmm . . .' goes my uncle.

Obviously, Aminata's tale doesn't interest my uncle much. So I ask:

'Is it far, your house?'

'Not that far if there weren't so many traffic jams.'

'Why aren't we going to the farm?'

She turns around, looks at me, lets out a deep sigh while vaguely shaking her head.

'Could well be I'm beginning to get too old to go on a real holiday. You either have to be young and full of piss and vinegar and ready to risk everything, or else you have to have lots of money. In France you can't venture out without dough.'

'But don't you have money?' I ask.

'Oh! Bad times will come soon enough, so you've got to look ahead.'

150

'If you were to get married . . .' begins uncle Kouam.

But then all of a sudden he stops speaking, as if he's seen a stop sign.

◆

Aminata's flat is large, almost as large as Lolita's. She has furniture made of white wood because she doesn't always clean and white hides the dust better, so she explained to me. She has whole collections of all kinds of animals on her curtains, too, and on her windows, and even on her tablecloth. 'That's to remember Africa by,' she told me laughingly. There are zebras, lions, giraffes, and kingfishers, and if you close your eyes very tightly, you can make believe you're in the middle of a virgin forest, only you're really in Paris, on the rue Montmartre. There are pictures of Allah, too. 'So he'll forgive me my sins,' she tells me. There is a toilet and a living-room just to receive her guests, people I do not know and never see more than once.

She gave me a room. My room looks out over a small garden in the back with a fountain and flowers. It's the first time ever that I have a room all to myself.

'That way you'll have the morning sun,' she says.

'It's great here,' I go. 'I really like it.'

'So much the better,' she answers. 'I think that . . .'

But she doesn't finish her sentence. Someone's at the door. She runs to open it. I follow her.

It's a man. A gentleman like you see on television. But this one here, as soon as I lay my eyes on him I know already that I don't like this guy. I don't like his way of walking, I don't like his teeth, I don't like his eyes, nor the way he's dressed. And besides he smells bad.

'Come in, come in,' she says.

But she needn't have bothered, he is already in the living room. He's wearing a suit of twilled flannel. He doesn't take his eyes off me.

'Who's that over there?' he asks Aminata.

'My son Mamadou.'

He lights a cigarette and continues to look at us as if he had something in the back of his mind. He is white, somewhat dark-

151

skinned, with grey eyes that are strangely cold when he stares at you. Wavy black hair and one of those moustaches that look as if they were drawn with a pen. He must have a problem with his left arm because he holds it away from his body. And when he brings his hand to his mouth to light a cigarette, his jacket gapes a bit. And I notice a leather strap across his chest. That must be a support for his arm. He looks at us again, then asks:

'He's not going to be living here, I hope?'

Aminata doesn't answer. And Monsieur Mohammed ben Sallah's eyes are colder than ever.

'Aminata, I thought I'd told you there would be no question of having a kid here.'

'All right, all right. It's only for a few days.'

'And how'll you do that? Who's going to look after the kid?'

'I'll manage.'

'I'll manage,' he repeats, watching her with an evil look. 'That's a good one! Playing the nanny . . . I'm your manager and it's up to me to tell you what's good for you.'

'The kid is staying,' Aminata answers. 'Only a few days. It's not a great drama! I'll manage.'

'And that's all you have to say! I'll manage . . . I'm not so fucking stupid that I'm gonna swallow that. If ever . . .'

Then he puts his hand inside his jacket and takes something out that he points at Aminata. It's a gun. Suddenly my bladder seems too full. But I don't feel like having a pee. I'm struck with helplessness. All I see is his eyes. A horrifying expression. I look at his eyes, then at the door. It seems a thousand miles away. Aminata is not concerned about Monsieur Mohammed's threats. She goes towards the bar. She fills a glass then turns around and asks:

'Will you have a drink?'

'No! Not until this kid gets the hell out of here.'

At that point, Monsieur Mohammed takes his gun and points it at me, just like that. He turns the safety catch of his gun as if to be sure that everything is working. I don't take my eyes off him. Then he licks his lips with his tongue.

'Stop! Will you?' she asks. 'Put away your toy or you'll frighten the boy.'

152

'You'll do as I say or you're dead!'

'You're the one who's dead, look at you!' she says with a big smile.

He puts away his gun, looking sheepish, and me, I go 'pfff'!

Aminata serves everyone. I'm allowed to have a nice icy cold Coke. Then she sits down, stretches out her legs and lights a cigarette. Monsieur Mohammed, all softened up, puts on some music and sits down as well. He looks at me and says:

'Nice flat, isn't it?'

'Yeah,' I answer.

'As soon as I saw it the first time, I knew this place would do Aminata a world of good. That's exactly what I was hoping for when I decided to handle her. This is where she can get the rest her profession requires. You've no idea, kid, how exhausting life is with the social obligations a young girl must meet if she wants to break into showbiz. Never a moment's relaxation. It's hard to get a start.'

Aminata agrees with a nod of her head.

'How right you are, Mohammed!'

'And then with the pollution in the city which undermines your health . . . In short, without this, she'd be done for.'

Aminata empties her glass and puts it back on a coffee table. She gets up and goes to the kitchen. She's reeling a little as she walks. I'm worried. She remains aloof. I have the feeling that she's homesick or something like that. Basically, I really like her, Aminata. I don't hold it against her that she abandoned me. Life had been rough on her. Monsieur Mohammed is explaining the hardships of her profession to me. That call upon every ounce of energy to create, which requires absolute availability, or something I didn't understand too well. Then he gets up without any warning and goes to the kitchen.

At that moment I hear Aminata's voice. She's yelling:

'I want you to leave me alone for a few days! I want some time with my son. If you want me to, I'll give you sixty per cent of what I take in. I don't give a shit! But I want some peace and quiet!'

'Calm down, pet. I'm saying it for your own good. You know, in this business it's enough not to be around for a week and you've lost the hang of it.'

'I don't intend to stop . . . I'm merely going to get organised, that's all!'

153

'Out of the question! Otherwise I'll go wild.'

'As you wish!'

He came back into the living room, he looked at me with those eyes of his that want to tear everything to shreds. He nodded to me and left. I didn't see him again.

Then we opened a bottle of champagne to celebrate the occasion. She had got all dressed up for the champagne, but the little rompers she has on now are just like the others, except that this pair is striped like a stick of barley sugar. She's wearing yellow sandals with a strap between her toes and her nails are bright red. She's wearing a wide, very heavy bracelet on her wrist, and a small golden chain around her ankle. She filled our glasses and we said cheers. We finished the champagne, I was sitting in an armchair next to her and feeling very much in my element.

'What's he got against you, that man?' I ask.

'Nothing, darling, don't worry.'

'If he ever hurts you, I swear I'll kill him.'

'Don't say that, Loukoum! Besides, when I have enough money we'll go far away from here together. We'll go to Canada.'

'What's that, Canada?'

'Canada? I'll tell you.' (She lights a cigarette and stretches her legs.) 'It's the biggest place in the world, and there isn't a single pimp other than a few Indians. I've been planning to go to Canada for years but I've never had enough money to get there. Once, right in the beginning, I wanted to go to Canada. I left here at the crack of dawn, didn't breathe for fear I'd lose my courage. But the more I thought about it, the more frightened I became, and before I'd done fifty miles, I backed out and turned around. I've never tried again since then.'

She's twirling her glass in her hands, then suddenly she gets up and says:

'Maybe it's better if . . .'

She goes to her room, brings back reams of paper. She takes a pencil, plays with figures, erases them, and recalculates.

'There's nothing to be done,' she says. 'Without cash you don't get very far. And you'd find yourself working in God only knows what kind of a dump doing any kind of work. They're not healthy, those places, I'm telling you.'

Then she takes a map of the world, traces a horizontal line. She does some more calculations, it's the same thing:

'We'd be without money round about Buenos Aires or Rio de Janeiro! It's not worth pursuing. We'll never make it! We'll find ourselves smack in the middle of the Amazonian forest. The only thing to do is to work hard for that son-of-a-bitch Mohammed and calmly wait until I've saved enough money . . . Good night, my darling.'

I went yippee! in my heart, because, to tell the truth, I didn't want to go anywhere without Lolita. So, I got up, I went to the door, I turned around to her and said:

'Don't fret about Canada, I'm going to take you there.'

I'm falling like a stone into a black well which is undoubtedly death.

In my head is emptiness or else a fat black cloud.

I've lost my memory. And what is all this for?

I have wives who'll end up strangling me in my sleep.

I have a son in whom I shall not be continued.

He has pushed his frontiers away. He has set up his world inside that world of yours, friend, which I cannot penetrate, for his nation, which is yours, friend, has been formed and protects itself jealously. A one-way street, I can no longer pass through.

Today, without any real kinship, without any love and full of remorse, my world is exploding in a burst of fire inside my skull.

Yet still within me, the vague impulses of a battle of a bygone era. From today onward, I want to ward off the threats of its completion. Very strong and very tall, I would prefer to keep everything in its place as my father before me, as my father's father before him. But there it is! A great wind disperses me, spatters me with hatred, with imperturbable logic closed upon my happiness. The era has chosen my end.

I looked at the sky, friend, just at the sky. There I read the text of a memory, but its consonants are missing, planted elsewhere, under a hut, inside a prison, in a forest.

I mentally list landscapes that are dead to me now, forms of behaviour that do not belong in my time.

Nothing belongs to me under this winter sky.

I write for the past. A slice of something that resembled a life. My life. I apply myself. A slice of life should express itself in a few lines. Despite my efforts, you will not understand my life. All the more so because somewhere a mistress, an intellectual, has spoken to you too explicitly about my feelings. And the mention of polygamy, of continu-

*ing a lineage, will confirm your judgement. A question of race. Or of
an era.*

I certainly would have deserved all that was going to follow . . .

(Abdou Traoré)

Aminata's room is on the other side, it looks out over the street and so
she can sell what she has to sell without putting herself out too much.
Aminata works late, she gets up late, as her profession requires. She
sleeps in silk sheets to keep her skin soft, seeing that's the basis of her
business and that without it she couldn't work. Her bed is wide and I
can understand why she doesn't often want to leave it.

'I'd like to go and live on the moon,' she says to me one day.

'Oh yeah?' I ask.

'You think that's stupid?'

'Not completely. There's too much shit on earth!'

'I've got it in my head,' she says.

I don't see where else a house like this might be. So I say nothing.

She goes on:

'I could take the stars and make my roof with them.'

'I see you've got it all figured out,' I tell her.

'Oh, my son, you, you're not so dumb.'

'What'll your house be made of?' I ask her.

'Air. You think that can't be done?'

'They've managed to build a train underneath the Channel.'

'Will you come and live with me?' she asks.

'I'll think about it,' I say.

And then she explains to me that using cement or even wooden
planks, as they do on earth, is not hygienic. And that asphalt and all
that is a killer for the lungs. She explains a ton of stuff to me. Maybe
I'll be a builder one day, but as I think about that more carefully, I
don't think I'd like that very much because that's for the Portuguese
because of how work is divided internationally.

'And if it rains in heaven, how will you protect yourself against
that?' I ask her.

'We'll put stones on it.'

157

'But they'll fall on our heads.'

'There's no heaviness,' she retorts. 'It just floats; so there.'

I don't understand, so I change the subject just as adults always do when they don't know what to answer.

'You won't have any flowers,' I tell her.

'I'll see them from above,' she answers. 'I'll be able to see the bougainvillaea.'

'And roses?'

'The roses too.'

'And mimosa?'

'All of that. Even the coral trees, the frangipani, the tulips, the animals, I'll see it all in one single sweep, without anyone there to give me any arguments.'

In short, she's having fun like a kid, which she isn't any more, and I am too.

As for the cooking, I won't talk about it. Better than M'am and Soumana put together in one single kitchen! She goes to market, she brings back fresh produce so as not to poison me with bio-chemistry. She sits down on a stool in the kitchen. She peels the vegetables, she cuts up the plantains, she takes the weevils out of the millet. She pounds it all, she lights the fire, and she cooks.

She is all for a structured schedule, since I'm living with her. As high noon strikes, wherever I may be, in front of the television or in my room, she calls me: 'Loukoum, it's ready'. All I have to do is put my feet underneath the table like a real gentleman. I gorge myself on chicken, beef, lamb. There are mangoes, too, guavas, custard-apples which she finds at the Chinese vendor on the corner who basically sells to black people only, I don't know why. I eat enough for four, I drink sodas, then I let out a belch to please her.

Afterwards we watch the news because it's always the same, seeing that mankind loves to wage war. Sometimes I'm afraid because you see disembowelled men, children who are guillotined, and all that. What I love are the libel cases in the court because that makes all the black folk talk and for a few days everyone forgets that we have false papers. But what I like above all is the happiness I enjoy with Aminata. It's true that I feel nothing any more while I'm happy. Sometimes, Aminata takes me to a café where you can have pistachio ice-cream.

There's nothing better than strawberry flavour. Before I really used to like coffee ice-cream. But since I found out about the prices of the raw materials that are imported cheaply from Africa, I no longer eat that stuff. A question of solidarity. Solidarity in the struggle of a people to decide for itself, as Monsieur Ndongala says.

Then Aminata goes off to work. But first she prepares dinner for me, which she puts in the refrigerator, and she cleans up the place quite thoroughly. She puts on short leather trousers, boots that come all the way up to her thighs, and a sweater with a rolled collar that fits closely around her breasts, since that is what a client notices first. She's gone all night and comes home in the morning, her eyes all red, with dreadful breath, all smelly, as if she'd spent the night with the homeless of Belleville.

◆

Sometimes, my uncle Kouam visits us. You'd think he'd lost his head, seeing that all he says is 'By gosh!' Today, my uncle Kouam came over to eat with us. After the meal, Aminata is singing. It's a song called 'Where are the men of our day?' My uncle looks at her while she sings, she bats her eyes just for him. My uncle arches his back as if he were a cat who's being caressed. He's practically purring. And then, he watches her, watches her, you'd think he's ready to swallow her whole without even having her cooked first. As for the seasoning, as is always the case with fine gourmets, he doesn't give it a thought. I can understand, for Aminata's dress is as pretty as a dying star and it shimmers in the sunlight with its red, yellow, and ochre sparkles. Her skin, too, shimmers and her teeth, you'd think she was going to bite into some chocolate or something else very sweet. As for me, they pay absolutely no attention to me. They're inside their wrappings of tenderness and they pay no attention to me. I purposely break a glass, but they don't even scold me. Just so you know. They look at each other, they smile at each other like the mental retards I saw in the bus the other day. Of course, they're not retarded, all this is just to let you know how truly, truly happy they are just to look at each other. Well, after all, it's not for me she's singing, but for their very own and slavish adult pleasure. Me, too, I look at Aminata. It's true that she's

159

beautiful and so is her dress. If she hadn't been my biological mother as they say, I do believe ... Well that's how it is and I can't do anything about it, nothing at all! And my heart shrinks. Why? Later, my uncle took her by the hand and they disappeared into the bedroom.

I picked up the telephone. I dialled Lolita's number. I knew it, Lolita's number. I had swiped it from school, from Mademoiselle Garnier's notebook.

'Hello, Lolita,' I said, because I recognised her voice right away.

'Who's this?'

'It's Mamadou.'

'Oh,' she goes.

Then she remained silent.

'Are you all right?' I asked just to say something.

'No, Mamadou. I'm leaving Belleville today. Mum says that this area isn't good for me.'

'No, Lolita,' I go. 'You're going to stay with me. We're leaving together.'

'How're we going to do that?'

'We'll get married.'

'But we have no money, Loukoum.'

'I'll find work.'

'You don't have a profession,' she says, 'and you're just a kid!'

'I'm a guy,' I say. 'And ...'

I have no time to finish my sentence when she cuts me off, sharply.

'There's my mum, Mamadou. I've got to hang up. I'll write to you.'

Then she hung up.

I'm trembling from head to foot. I flop down on the couch. Tears are rolling down my cheeks. I don't know what to think any longer.

Someone is touching me gently, touching my shoulders and calling me: 'Loukoum, Loukoum,' very gently.

It's Aminata calling me. She caresses my head, then asks:

'Why're you crying, son?'

I say nothing.

'Aren't you happy here with me?'

'Of course I am,' I answer.

'Do you want me to sing something for you? A lullaby?'

I don't answer.

160

So she began to sing in Malinke. I don't understand a word of what she's singing, but it's sweet, very sweet, so much so that I feel like going to sleep.

'What does it say?' I ask her.

'It's the story of a woman who loses her child and wanders around looking for him.'

'Like you?' I ask her.

'If you want,' she says.

I look at her, and it is as if Lolita is there before me, singing just for me alone, just to make me happy.

◆

My dad gave Aminata permission to keep me another week. Aminata is very happy. And I am, too. My uncle Kouam comes every day. He keeps her company wherever she wants to go. You'd think he was a puppydog, following behind her with his tongue hanging out. At night, they sleep in the same bed and I hear noise that sounds a little like teeth grinding. I wonder what they could be doing to be making sounds like that. And right into the early hours of the morning, on my word of honour!

The first time my uncle Kouam slept at the house, Aminata asked me at breakfast:

'Are you fond of your uncle Kouam?'

'As much as everyone else,' I answered.

'Hmm, hmm,' she went.

She kept silent, then looked at me with strange eyes:

'Would you like him to be your dad?'

'I already have a dad,' I answered. 'You don't need my permission to do what you need to do with him,' I said.

'What do you think I do with him?'

I didn't answer, but that didn't prevent me from thinking she could sleep with the entire world, I wouldn't toady up to them.

The third day, I asked her:

'Do you want to have another baby?'

My heart beat loudly inside my chest and I waited for her answer. She giggled and then said:

161

'For me, I think, that's all over.'

'When you sleep with someone, you get pregnant,' I told her.

'Yeah, but I'm on the pill.'

'You really love him, uncle Kouam?'

'That means nothing for a black woman.'

'Oh really?' I ask as if out of curiosity.

'Yeah. A black woman, she chooses the man who does her the least harm, end of story, that's all.'

'You like sleeping with him?' I ask again.

'At your age, Loukoum, you ought not to be asking questions like that.'

I didn't dare tell her I knew so many things already, my childhood is long gone.

So I take my pencil and I draw a woman. She's like the moon with a little man who's working inside her belly. While I'm drawing, Aminata is humming something. Her song was awfully sad. Suddenly she stops singing, looks at me with the eyes of a beaten dog:

'Gotta go,' she says looking at her watch. 'Work's waiting.'

She gets up, takes her bag, and asks me:

'You need any money?'

I don't answer. I look down. And continue drawing.

'You're a terrific boy, you know? Your drawing is fantastic.'

'Oh, it's easy when you've nothing to do with your time.'

'Are you bored? I thought you were having a good time?'

'Of course, mum.' (It's the first time I've called her 'mum' and it feels funny.) 'But soon I have to go back to school.'

She looks at me. She strokes my head. It's nice and a pity. I'm thinking of my dad, of M'am and of Soumana, and I'm thinking how it's really a pity.

◆

I went back home. Soumana is no longer there. Nobody talks about it. Nothing. Wiped away. I don't dare ask any questions. My sister Fatima has nightmares. She howls. She wakes up the whole house. She says she's just seen her mum in heaven with a head made of light. She cries. My dad takes her in his arms and comforts her. My dad has changed a

162

lot. Now he helps M'am with the children and in the kitchen, too. You'd think he'd grown millions of years older in two weeks. It's as if something has happened on earth that caused him not to be the same any more. He talks to M'am with respect and sometimes he caresses her, just like that, like little kisses on her neck. I've never seen him do that before. He often speaks to her kindly, but you'd think M'am didn't believe in it too much. So she bursts out laughing and pulls away.

Mademoiselle Esther comes to see us frequently. Her bulge up front. Her body in the middle. Her bag behind. She flops down in my dad's chair breathing heavily. The mountain watches television. She takes off her shoes. She stretches her legs. M'am serves her little cakes, raisins, doughnuts, broth, fish with rice ... But she turns it all down with disdain.

'You want something else? What shall I fix up for you?' M'am asks.

'I want strawberries.'

M'am goes downstairs to buy strawberries. Mademoiselle Esther no longer wants them. She calls for chocolate. M'am complies without balking. My dad sighs. He says nothing. He lets all her whims go by so as not to annoy the baby.

Today, Mademoiselle Esther is truly in a murderous mood. M'am has made her soy beans, highly seasoned, the way she likes them. But she pushed the tray away without a word. For a moment, she remained motionless. Her eyes were staring at the ceiling. Her bulge was moving up and down, her hands were folded on top. Then she began to cry and, concerned, my dad asked:

'Aren't you well?'

She shakes her head.

'The baby?'

'You hate me, don't you?' she asked.

'I don't hate you,' my dad replied.

'Then why don't you ever touch my belly? Nobody likes pregnant women,' she groaned. 'I can see it clearly. On the street, in the stores, everywhere. People passing by are looking me up and down all the time. It's horrible!'

'It's all in your head,' my dad goes. 'Everyone is very fond of you.'

'And Kaba, he used to be so nice to me. Now he doesn't look at me any more.'

163

'That's not important,' my dad says.

'It's terribly important!'

She began to cry even more. M'am quickly came from across the kitchen without a word. She took Mademoiselle Esther in her arms, stroked her hair, then asked my dad angrily:

'Now what have you done to her, poor little thing?'

'Nothing at all. She says nobody loves her.'

'And naturally you didn't reassure her?'

'I said she was wrong.'

'Oh you, I know you! You're such a moron.'

'I . . .'

'Shut up. After everything you've done.'

'Me? But I haven't done a thing!'

M'am looked at him. Her eyes were hard, hard, wide with anger. You'd think that her feelings for my dad were crumbling. Then she kissed Mademoiselle Esther's forehead.

'I'm so unhappy,' Mademoiselle Esther said in a plaintive voice.

M'am hugged her shoulders even tighter.

'Don't worry, little one. M'am is taking care of everything. That guy does nothing but make trouble. I don't know how I've managed not to leave him.'

Dad clenched his fingers very tightly, but he said nothing.

◆

At school it's no longer the same since Lolita isn't there any more. Sure enough, Pierre Pelletier is nice to me, and patient like no other person on God's whole earth. Sometimes, he teaches me things, for instance that the first people existed easily five thousand years ago, he talks to me about *homo sapiens* or something like that, something I didn't understand too well. He also corrects my French so that I'll become something other than a street sweeper in France, even if, as the name indicates, it is necessary to have them, otherwise France would stink. He says you must pronounce the words carefully and that a sentence always needs a subject, a verb and an object.

'All that isn't really important,' I say to him.

'Oh yes, it is!' he tells me. 'If you don't change the way you speak, nobody is going to take you seriously.'

'But me, all I ask from life is to be happy,' I retort.

'Still, you'll be a lot more comfortable with yourself,' he says.

Nothing can make me feel good without Lolita. That's what's wrong with my body, my blood, my soul, but I don't tell anyone. Now every time I speak my way, Pierre Pelletier corrects me so that I'll become a gentleman he says. Afterwards, I feel as if my head is empty, as if I know nothing any more. Then everything gets all muddled.

He's given me a whole stack of books to read. He says that way I'll get on. Allah! It's pretty difficult! But I like reading. And one day while I'm here reading, Madame Saddock, whom you've already had the pleasure of meeting, comes sailing in. She's dressed like a white lady with a pleated skirt and a white shirt and matching shoes. She sails in and asks for Soumana straight out.

'She's gone back to Africa,' M'am tells her.

Madame Saddock frowns and says, looking as if she doesn't believe this:

'That's strange . . . In her letter . . .'

'What letter?' asks M'am.

'Yeah, what letter?' asks my dad.

'A letter.'

'But what was she saying in her letter?' asks M'am.

'I don't owe you any explanation. But it is strange.'

'If you don't want to say anything, Madame,' says my dad, 'it's that there is no letter.'

'Are you calling me a liar?'

'I didn't say that. But, since . . .'

'I know about you!' Madame Saddock threatens. 'You mistreated her!'

'But . . .'

'And you've killed her!'

'You're mad! Get out, leave my house immediately.'

Madame Saddock sniggers, then she says:

'Fine, fine . . . I'm going . . . But you'll be hearing from me very soon.'

I have gone mad. Besides, they've come for me. No, don't cry over me, friend. Weep for yourself, for your son. Today I know what it means to be here, locked up. I knew that other folks were here, locked up, away from the world, but I never would have had such a clear, such a precise image of it.

I thought I felt anguish. Now I am touching it.

I thought I was afraid. Now I am afraid.

I thought I was defeated. Now I am defeated.

My certainties are taking flight.

My head is exploding.

Don't think. Every man makes mistakes. Every man walks ahead of his own ruin. Everyone errs! But I've done nothing wrong. I have only tried to find suitable ways of dispelling evil in an environment that's different.

Allah will come to my rescue. Stay calm. Master my anguish and reflect slowly. I have to force myself to believe that nothing serious is happening, that nothing serious can happen, until the fatal knot will come untied in the same way it was tied.

I have to be calm and feel calm. I have done nothing wrong. It was the only recipe for warding off the evil spells. But minute manipulations require delicate preparations. It would have been necessary not to make errors in plants, dosages, the right moment or temperature.

I made no mistakes. I only sought survival within signs of my own. But you were afraid, friend. You are afraid of this God who is so different, of my ideas which are so different from the intentions of mankind, you are afraid of suffering, of death, of everything that according to my traditions is given to us as something good but which for you would be the pinnacle of horror.

I have done nothing wrong, it's your legislation that has not integrated my customs.

(*Abdou Traoré*)

Lord! The police came to get my dad. It was quite a dramatic turn of events. And he seemed to have no idea what was happening to him. They put handcuffs on him and took him away. M'am didn't budge. She clenched her fists very tight. Her face is pure despair. But she says nothing. It was only when she heard no more sounds that she collapsed. She weeps and weeps and weeps. Life is pitiless. Then she calms down. Then she says:

'Even in her grave she doesn't let go of me.'

◆

Then the journalists arrived. They placed us like this, the littlest ones up front and M'am behind us.

'Smile . . . Come on, a little smile!' the photographer said.

But no one felt like smiling. They took pictures anyway. They left. And today there is a big photo of us in the newspaper. Alexis showed it to me. And it says: 'A FAMILY OF IMMIGRANTS REGISTERS FALSE BIRTHS AND DIVERTS SEVERAL MILLION CENTIMES TO FAMILY BENEFITS.'

'Now you're famous!' says Alexis, laughing.

Personally, I could have done without it very nicely. I feel a vague melancholy. I don't know what's wrong with me, but I'm not feeling well. I watch television but I see nothing, I hear nothing. You'd think there were too many things inside my eyes clogging up my sight. I zap it. So then, to pass the time, I started writing. I'm writing a real book. About my life and one day, I tell myself, they'll make a film out of it.

◆

They're still holding my dad. Monsieur Ndongala and the whole black gang are visiting us. Monsieur Ndongala says they can't keep my dad

167

much longer, since they have no proof. But my uncle Kouam maintains that it's only a fuss about a nigger so you can't tell, it's not of any real interest to white people. If they had capital punishment, they would have executed him and that's that.

I don't know what to make of it any more. I don't understand what my dad has done wrong, so . . .

Madame Saddock came to see us. She tried to explain a whole lot of stuff to Ma'm. That she'd done this for their own good. That my dad was a bastard. That he didn't deserve a single woman in the world . . . But M'am wanted to have none of it, and threw her out of the house on the spot. It was really funny.

There's not much left to eat at home, there's no more money, seeing as my dad is the one who's always called upon and kept around so they can clean him out. I'm making bracelets, I sell them, and give the money to M'am.

'Keep your money,' she says to me. 'You'll need it for something else.'

I insist, she accepts but, she says, on condition that she takes part in the business. So in the beginning she helps me a little. Soon she begins to enjoy it and directs the enterprise. She orders lots of snakeskins from Africa. One day she says:

'We could make rings, too.'

We make rings. We earn money. And Ma'm is really pleased. Moreover she has the extraordinary idea of hiring a white man to swindle other white men, nothing could be better if you want my opinion. The white man is big with a moustache. He is young and has no respect for black women because he's had plenty of them, in the rue Saint-Denis, at a hundred francs a session. He always says: 'There's nothing better than a black arse! There's nothing better than a black arse!' One day, when he starts that with M'am, she looked at him, then said to him: 'Go wipe your behind first, then!' He was put in his place nicely and me, I laughed my head off.

I am the man of the house. I sit down in my dad's armchair after work. It's really neat. M'am serves me tea. She sits down next to me and tells me stories. She talks about dad, her marriage, my sisters, me. Simple things of everyday life. I've become so used to making braided jewellery that I'm mixing colours just to see what I can come up with.

Outside, life goes on and it's all right, except for the business with Lolita which keeps me from sleeping.

◆

Today, Mademoiselle Esther paid us a visit. She's had her baby. She has more of a belly than before, but she's still very beautiful. She brought her little boy. His name is Abdou Junior. And that's where it all went wrong with M'am.

'A real sweetie,' Mademoiselle says as she sticks him right under M'am's nose. 'At the clinic everyone was crazy about him.'

M'am continues to shell her peanuts without looking at her.

'You wouldn't want to adopt him by any chance?'

M'am says nothing. Mademoiselle Esther could be there or not, it wouldn't make the slightest bit of difference. So much so that I suddenly understood why M'am always used to say that when you are sad it's in the eyes. Hers were like knives.

'I'm making you a present of a child and you don't even answer! Why?'

At that point, M'am threw her peanuts on the mat. The gesture alone contained a great many things. It was the past and the present. She lets out a deep sigh and looks at Mademoiselle Esther and Abdou Junior.

'One kid more or less, what difference would that make to you?'

M'am pulls her braids together and shapes a clump on the top of her head.

'You're not answering me, because you are jealous,' Mademoiselle Esther goes. 'He resembles Abdou. You can tell it's his blood!'

'I'd rather say you are the jealous one,' M'am responds to her. 'I never asked you to make me any kids. I don't want any!'

'Why not?'

''Cause I'm fed up with Abdou's mistresses and with his foolishness. I do not need a child, is that clear?'

'But you love Loukoum! He's not your son, as far as I know!'

'Just as you said. I'm tired of raising other people's kids. Loukoum, that's different. Fate entrusted him to me, full stop, that's all.'

'Abdou Junior will love you, too, you know?'

169

'And how will you manage that miracle?' M'am asks her.

'I'll raise him to have respect for both men and women.'

'Dream on,' M'am says.

Mademoiselle Esther looks at me. She doesn't believe her ears. Tears well up in her eyes and her voice is trembling.

'Well then, see you another time.'

'Never, I hope,' M'am says.

'I do thank you for everything,' Mademoiselle Esther says.

'Don't mention it,' M'am went.

She left.

M'am didn't feel too well. Her eyes were wet, too. Once Mademoiselle had left, she said:

'Where, dear Lord, can I get a rest from my suffering?'

I had no idea.

And then she spat.

Don't think. Don't think. Above all don't think about anything. What has happened is in the past. Don't think. Don't think so much. Stay calm. It's enough to prop your head up there, yes, like that. You are comfortable there, head propped up, yes, like that. You can close your eyes, reopen them, it all amounts to the same thing. It's the same. As you open your eyes, you discover the walls, torn apart by a few imprisoned hands. You can also draw by scratching the whitewash little by little with your nails. You scratch slowly because you have endless time ahead of you. Bit by bit you scrape away and the unpleasant little noise of your nail against the wall, that screeching sound that sets your teeth on edge, and the nail sliding across the wall reveals a drawing that little by little takes on a human form. No, half human, and it keeps you company. Because the moment arrives when the image loosens itself from the naked wall, because finally there comes a moment when the awkwardly drawn form resembles something. A fish? A monkey? A man? A woman. Yes, a woman certainly, who begins to look at you, fixes her large eyes filled with wonder upon you, and it seems that you're no longer alone.

Don't think, don't think. I must watch the wall, let time flow as I watch the wall. You must not think, because you can't straighten anything out while you're thinking. No. You are here, calm, still. You are good, you wanted to do good. You wanted to do the right thing. Everything you've done, you've done well. You weren't thinking of evil. You did it as well as you knew how, the best you could. If it were to be done over again . . .

No! Idiot.

Don't think.

Destiny's inevitability, resign yourself! You must stay here, calm, as

171

long as necessary, without budging. Learn to concentrate little by little in a vacuum without thought. As long as I am here, very calm, nothing can happen to me. Besides, I cannot do anything by myself. Calm. I cannot do anything, so I cannot make mistakes. What will happen will happen beyond my power, without me. Besides, you had no choice. French legislation anticipated it all. Except for this. Two or four wives. Idiot! Stay calm. Imperturbable. He who shows his mind to be lucid, who proves his wholeness, can say that he is triumphant, even if the whole world believes he's peeing in his pants. He triumphs if he maintains a core of freedom which allows him to choose what will happen to him, what will crush him.

I want that! I want that!

(Abdou Traoré)

They let my dad go. He didn't get his job back at the sanitation department. He says it's not a problem, and that anyway he prefers to be helping us make jewellery. It's more pleasant work.

Monsieur Kaba asked him if it didn't bother him that his wife is in charge.

'Why should that bother me?' he said. 'It seems to please her. She knows the business and she's a good teacher. I'm learning to manage quickly.'

It bothered me a little when he took his armchair back. It was almost like a shock. But he is so nice that well, after all, he is my dad. And he truly is not the same any more. On the nights of the full moon, he stands at the window, dreaming, and looks at the man in the moon. I don't know what goes on in his head. It doesn't interest M'am at all. You'd think it is she who no longer sees him. He does everything. He helps M'am with the cooking on Sundays. Then he takes her for walks in the park. M'am no longer has the same appearance. She wears trousers, blue, yellow, red ones with matching sandals. She looks younger, more carefree. My dad, he's looking for something. You'd think he was studying nature. The other day he brought a plant home. He's taking care of it, feeds it, as if it were a baby. He even brought flowers home for M'am. Monsieur Guillaume says he's looking for

God in woman. He buys plenty of jewellery for M'am and never lets a chance go by of paying her a compliment as if he thinks she's very beautiful. M'am doesn't listen to him. You'd think it was a frog talking to her, so she doesn't hear it. Sometimes she bursts out laughing and talks about something else. For example, that it's really quite hot and that she'd really like to learn how to swim or to go dancing. So then my dad gets worried. I've heard my dad say to Monsieur Guillaume he doesn't know what to do next. That he really loves her. And Monsieur Guillaume told him that the best thing is to talk to her again. My dad went: 'Great! I'll ask her to marry me a second time,' and everyone applauded.

Me, I don't worry about all this, for I have many questions that bother me a great deal. I wonder why love makes us suffer? Why the earth is round? Why are there stars? Why laughter, trouble, and joy? Why the different races? What purpose does it all serve, these differences that hurt and cause so much uproar? I realise that school has taught me many things without ever giving answers to what is essential. I still have quite a bit of work to do.

I think of Lolita. I'm sad. I'm unhappy. Especially when I see a girl walking along and I think it's her. I remember her hair, the rain outside, the rain beating down, her fingers running round, cuddly fingers. I remember everything. And everything comes back. At times, I don't want to think any more. I want her to leave me. I want her to let me breathe. I'm exhausted. I want to live as I did yesterday. As I did before that day. I have to shake myself so then I work. I live for my work. I write non-stop. But I'm happy with my lot. If Lolita writes to me, I'll be in seventh heaven. If she doesn't write to me, I'll make do with my lot among my parents, the black people of Belleville, and school. Keep your mind busy while you wait, I tell myself. That's what I have to learn about life: to fill the gap.

I'm in the middle of these thoughts when I receive a letter from Lolita. Life is really strange! I opened the envelope. Then I closed it again. My hands were shaking.

At night I can't get to sleep. I tell myself the story of Lolita from every angle. I pull it out of my head again. I get lost in my own tale. Begin at the beginning! Begin at the end and end with the beginning. Yes, our story begins with this letter. I haven't read it. I don't dare.

Maybe she's telling me she no longer loves me. She can't stand me any more.

Stretched out in my bed, I look at the ceiling. I listen to the sounds of the night and I think of Lolita. Some young people passed by. They were laughing loudly. I hear noises coming from the bed in the corner. My dad says he can't manage to fall asleep. That it's hot. That he's going to melt like a piece of sugar in the sun.

M'am gets up and opens the window. My dad says:

'Look at the moon, my love. You see the man in the moon?'

'Yeah,' M'am goes. 'Seems to me he's being punished and is working so that God will forgive him his crimes towards women.'

'I've hurt you a lot, haven't I?'

'Not me, Abdou. Yourself.'

'I know. Sooner or later everything you do turns against you. But now today I know you're frail, that you need protection.'

'You've noticed?'

'Of course! You, you're like a leaf. You'd think any minute the wind is going to blow you away. It was even worse when you were very young!'

'Still, that didn't stop you from . . .'

'Let's not talk about that, please?'

'As you wish.'

'Me, I want only one thing.'

'What, Abdou?'

'I'd like you to become my wife again, if I haven't broken everything in your heart.'

'I don't have any feelings any more, Abdou. It's as if I'm dead.'

'Give me at least one last chance.'

My dad falls silent before he continues:

'Sou's death has given me something to think about.'

'So much the better,' goes M'am.

'Yeah. I began to sense other deaths, you understand? And prison only reinforced this new view of life I have.'

'I see.'

'I'm learning to appreciate better the joy of having a wife like you and of having our children, too. I love them. I love you.'

'Well, if you love us, everybody will love you the way you deserve to be loved. That's the very principle of life.'

'Yeah. But tell me, woman, one day will you forgive me for all the pain I've caused you?'

Then I heard M'am weep.

◆

I get out of bed, Lolita's letter in my hands. My body is drifting, as is my mind. I see faces floating by as well. All the faces I have known in my life. I no longer hear anything. As if a glass partition were separating me from them. I no longer communicate. The bond is broken. The world has flown away. I open Lolita's letter.

> *Dear Mamadou,*
>
> *Maybe you think I've died. But I'm alive and thinking of you. I don't know whether I can write to you every day because they really check up on us here. There's a doctor who comes to see me every day. It seems that what happened between us will torment me for a long time to come yet, and that I will have nightmares at night.*
>
> *But when I sleep at night, I see you. You take my hand and you take me far away to a country where there is a lot of sun, many trees, lilac forests, bougainvillaeas, clowns who do magic tricks. In any case, I don't tell my dreams to anybody. Not even to Mum, who's worried about my health because I don't want to talk to her. Nobody knows a thing and they never will. They say I'm mentally ill. But I, I know you're there and nobody else can see you . . . Maybe I won't see your face for another hundred years, but I am sure that some day I shall see your face again.*
>
> *Your loving Lolita*

Lord! when I finish reading Lolita's letter, my whole body is hot. I'm beginning to spin around and around. I can't stay in one place. I raise my arms to the sky. Thank you, Lord, for having given me Lolita. Then I sit down in a corner, put my head on my knees. I weep. I imagine Lolita all alone in her bed. She stays awake for the same reasons. I weep some more. I'm dripping with tears. Lord! Yes, we'll be married! We'll have kids! I'll make them rooms with elephants, hippopotamuses, birds and flowers ... There'll be sunsets as on the holy pictures. With a large opening that sends you towards the gap in the heavens ...

For one moment I thought of Soumana; nobody talks about her, and yet she's here in every object, in every breath of air that goes through the house. Oh! God, there's some wild stuff that happens among blacks ...

Today is the fourteenth of July. The French had their Revolution. The entire tribe decided to go and have a picnic in the Bois de Boulogne. It's a holiday. So the blacks get together to make their own celebration. In the park, the bark on the trees is like the skin of an old elephant dancing in the heat of memories. A crushing heat. Children who scream. Mums who watch over the kids out of the corner of their eyes while serving food on paper plates.

Aminata and my uncle arrive. Her mouth is swollen. He's devouring her with his eyes. My uncle is happy from what I can see from his look.

Aminata throws herself into everyone's arms. She says:

'We're getting married, Kouam and I.'

M'am raises her head. Her eyes devour the couple with their arms around each other, then she asks:

'And your manager?'

'Pfff! I dropped him.'

'Mmmmm,' M'am goes.

My dad is looking out above the trees. He seems to be thinking and asks:

'Aren't you two afraid of reprisals? With pimps you never know, sometimes they find you on the bottom of the River Seine.'

'No problem,' says Aminata. 'I can't deal with life if we're here only to be unhappy.'

'I don't know how many men you've had,' says M'am. 'But I think you handle things rather well.'

'Yeah. Even misfortune wears itself out,' Aminata answers.

Her fixed stare turns to me. I close my eyes. I open them again. I look at the sky. I think that no matter where she is, Lolita is sharing this bit of sky with me. That fills me with happiness. I smile.

'What are you laughing about like a silly goose?' M'am asks jokingly.

176

I don't answer. She won't understand. They won't understand. They're not up on things. They're too old. And yet, they are so happy! . . .

Yes, the paths of happiness are very complicated.

THE AFRICAN WRITERS SERIES

The book you have been reading is part of Heinemann's long-established series of African fiction. Details of some of the other titles available in this series are given below, but for a catalogue giving information on all the titles available in this series and in the Caribbean Writers Series write to:
Heinemann Educational Publishers,
Halley Court, Jordan Hill, Oxford, OX2 8EJ.
United States customers should write to:
Heinemann, 361 Hanover Street,
Portsmouth, NH0381–3912, USA

BIYI BANDELE-THOMAS
The Man Who Came in from the Back of Beyond

Maude, a strange schoolteacher, tells the tale of a man from his girlfriend's past. As the naive student Lakemf listens, a tale of incest and revenge slowly begins to unfold.

CHENJERAI HOVE
Shadows

As the war for liberation rages around them, two young Zimbabweans must decide whether they will continue to live and love in such a barren land. A telling portrait of rural life and the strictures of colonial law.

NIYI OSUNDARE
Selected Poems

This collection contains the very best of Osundare's poetry. The verse testifies to his commitment to a popular 'total poetry' – words to be listened to in conjunction with song, dance and drumming.

TIYAMBE ZELEZA
Smouldering Charcoal

Two couples live under the rule of a repressive regime, and yet their lives seem poles apart. In this compelling study of growing political awareness, we witness the beginnings of dialogue between a country's urban classes.

NGŨGĨ WA THIONG'O
Secret Lives

A new edition of Ngũgĩ's collection of early stories revealing his increased political disillusionment and foreshadowing the novels which have made him one of Africa's foremost commentators.

ALEX LA GUMA
In the Fog of the Season's End

This is the story of Beukes – lonely, hunted, determined – working for an illegal organisation, and of Elias Tekwane, captured by the South African police and tortured to death in the cells.

CHARLOTTE BRUNER (ED)
The Heinemann Book of African Women's Writing

A companion piece to the earlier *Unwinding Threads*, also edited by Charlotte Bruner, this anthology of writing of the post colonial era provides new insights into a complex world.

CHINUA ACHEBE & C. L. INNES (EDS)
The Heinemann Book of Contemporary African Short Stories

This anthology displays the variety, talent and scope to be found in contemporary African writing. The collection includes work written in English and translations of francophone stories. The magical realism of Kojo Laing and Mia Couto contrasts with the styles of Nadine Gordimer, Ben Okri and Moyez Vassanji.

AMECHI AKWANYA
Orimili

Orimili takes his name from the great river that flows through his home town of Okocha. But while the river flows on to the wider world beyond, Orimili is anchored to his home town, and yearns to push his roots yet further in. His ambition is to be accepted in the company of elders, to wear the thick white thread of office round his ankle.

NURUDDIN FARAH
Sardines

In this stylish Somalian novel, Farah depicts the life of a woman living under the rule of Islam.

NADINE GORDIMER
Crimes of Conscience: Selected Short Stories

Set in her native Southern Africa, Gordimer's powerful collection reveals the misery of repression and coercion for both blacks and whites.

GAELE SOBOTT-MOGWE
Colour Me Blue

A strong collection of short stories reflecting daily life in Southern Africa. The author writes movingly, both about social injustices and the problems of personal relationships.

SEMBÈNE OUSMANE
Black Docker
(translated from the French by Ros Schwartz)

Set in Senegal in the Fifties, Diaw Falla, a docker whose real love is writing, meets Ginette Tontisanne. Her good connections ensure he is published – but under her name.

ALIFA RIFAAT
Distant View of a Minaret
(translated from the Arabic by Denys Johnson-Davies)

A hidden, private world, regulated by the call of the mosque, is depicted here. Frank and powerful, the novel conveys the frustrations of everyday life in Egypt for women in purdah.

AGNES SAM
Jesus is Indian and Other South African Stories

The great-granddaughter of an indentured labourer from India, Agnes Sam draws on her South African childhood and Indian past in this short story collection.

JACK MAPANJE
The Chattering Wagtails of Mikuyu Prison

A collection of poems condemning the Malawian regime that sends Mapanje to prison, but also celebrating the love of family and friends during this period.

BESSIE HEAD
The Collector of Treasures

A book of tales about the people in a Botswanan village, and their myths and legends.

WOLE SOYINKA (ED)
Poems of Black Africa

An extensive anthology of African poetry, collected by one of Africa's major poets.

HAMA TUMA
The Case of the Socialist Witchdoctor and Other Stories

A series of dark tales about the Ethopian big brother state where nothing is what it seems.

M. G. VASSANJI
Uhuru Street

Depicting the shops and tenements of Uhuru Street in Dar es Salaam in Tanzania from the innocent time of the colonial 1950s to the shattering 1980s, this is an evocative collection of short stories.

KENJO JUMBAM
The White Man of God

A charming novel about Tansa, whose Cameroonian village becomes divided by the arrival of a missionary, the 'white man of God'.